ASTRA
FISIC

Twelve Short Stories

sister alies therese

To order additional copies of this book, contact:
Bookwhip
1-855-339-3589
https://www.bookwhip.com

Also By
sister alies therese

'THE HOMERS OF CORK FORGE'

'HOME SWEET HOME'

'IN THE DARKNESS, Shine'

'not-for-sale'

'COMING SOON: A CUP OF COMFORT'

'CONTEMPLATIVE DRAWING AND
THE GIFTS OF MERCY'

CONTENTS

Astra Fisic and the Three Grumpy Sisters

Sarahfinna, Melodious and Whiplash gathered every Sunday morning at the *Uptown Downtown Only One In Town MAIN STREET Café* (usually referred to as *Thee Café.*) and had breakfast. These three, by town standards, were grumpy. They did not consider themselves so, because they had reasons, good reasons. The highlight of the morning was the hook- up with Astra Fisic their dear friend to talk over the news of the week and any other topic that might be relevant. Astra Fisic was an astronomer, slightly retired. She almost always wore a red hat.

They discussed politics, all sides. They discussed religion, all types. They discussed birds, all kinds. They discussed science, any kind. They discussed men, as many as possible. And they discussed death, as little as possible.

Sarahfinna was 59; Melodious was 62; and Whiplash was 65. Astra Fisic was, well no one was quite sure, maybe 60- something or even 80! Naw. Folks figured she was not quite sure herself.

The reason for grumpiness in each one was very different. Sarahfinna, besides being the youngest sister, had an acidic stomach.

She loved fried squirrel. Melodious, the middle girl, was tone deaf. She loved okra swimming in a pot of stew. Whiplash, the eldest, was accident-prone. She loved game pie, full-o-possum. And they all loved vinegar pie and so did Astra Fisic, who was not related. She was not grumpy. She did however, have her own issues!

It was a high summer-Sunday, already hot and muggy at 8am and all they could hope for was that Thee Café had good A/C going. Cool, real cool was needed. The sisters had gathered in their favorite spot, a large booth where they still had to squash and squeeze to get in, leaving just a little spot for Astra Fisic.

Astra Fisic was not there yet. Sarahfinna wanted to order breakfast (they always waited for each other) because her stomach was bubbling like a witches cauldron and the acid crept up her throat. Icky. Melodious was listening to some music on her headset and unfortunately for everyone else was loudly singing along. Whiplash had tripped twice already, once coming in on that old bit of rubber rug she *always* tripped on and then over a chair leg not quite under the neighboring table. She did not fall but caught the edge of the table. Yea! Astra Fisic was late.

Now that's something to be grumpy about. Each one agreed. They had their reasons and no one ought to try to change their minds. If you have a good reason, well, then, who says you can't be grumpy? Not even Astra Fisic. Oh, where is that girl? She had a very good memory, so she would know it was Sunday. It was that time of day, and she always ate breakfast. She went to Church much later. Gotta wonder.

They never started a 'real' conversation until Astra Fisic showed up because then they would have to start over. They thought Astra Fisic had the best topics. Like when she talked all that confusing stuff about the stars and planets. Well, who knew anything about all that? Well, Astra Fisic did. So they waited. You had to order your own food so no waitress bothered them.

"Did you talk to her this week?"

"Nope, not me," Whiplash responded. Melodious didn't actually hear the question. Her ears were covered with her headset and filled with the blues. She loved the parts where *he- left- her —and- she-ran -away —and- he —came- back -and -then they- got- married. BooHoo...* or something like that.

"Whaddaya think we ought to do?" Whiplash asked Sarahfinna.

"Don't know." She really didn't know.

Sarahfinna was thinner than she had been over the years. Melodious? Portly, bootie and boobs. Whiplash was well, just fat. These were perfectly good reasons for being grumpy they thought.

Whiplash had a hard time with clothes so she just wore old T-shirts and sweat pants. They stretched around most of her. She had a very pleasant smile though, but because she was always tripping or hurting herself, she did not show it too often. She had shoe issues.

Melodious tried every bra that the BIG RED STORE had and none fit properly so she just bobbled and bounced along, not caring what anyone else thought. She liked those sleazy running pants, long or short, and her bottom spread nicely into the soft material.

Sarahfinna had no issue here. She was just, well, average size for a 6' woman. She loved scarves and socks.

Before Astra Fisic arrives the three usually talk about who is walking into Thee Café and where they decide to sit and then, if they can see properly, what they ordered. For example, Whiplash noticed old Mr. Donald. Now he came in every day, wearing a different ball cap. He was a real collector, maybe 85, and sporting a small go-tee. He always tried to sit in the same small booth over near the candy shelves. Frequently it was full up and he was not too happy. He had the same problem when he went to Church. He liked a certain pew but those other thoughtless people got there first. Today's ball cap supported the *Yankees*. As far as Whiplash knew, he'd not been to NYC nor did he favor baseball. She knew he was a football fan. Never mind. His business. Today he was

3

eating a tall-stack, as Thee Café advertised. He had plenty of blueberry syrup and butter, no matter the report from the doctor.

And there was Ms. Tucker, former maid at the local *Friendly*MOTEL. That motel had been there for donkey's years and so had Ms. Tucker. She went to work there as a young woman after getting out of prison where she had served for four and a half years for, well no one was quite sure and she was not forthcoming. She always wore an apron as if she was ready to get back to work, but she had retired over three years ago. Guess it made her feel wanted or something. Sarahfinna thought it very odd indeed. Today she sported a very large sunhat decorated with feathers and flowers of purple and lilac. Some sparkly netting fell behind and it was stunning. The rest of her outfit was as boring as the hat was exciting. Along with the apron, she wore comfort shoes and a plain skirt with a broad silver belt.

There were the balding-boy-twins, now in their 40's who had only gone to school for three or four years and then stayed home and learned how to shell peas and cut corn. Eric and Eddie wore rough clothing all the time. Melodious said it was because that was the way their mama dressed them as children and they didn't know no better. They could drive a tractor, well Eric could, and they could bale hay and pick cotton. Mostly year round they looked like they had just come off the field. Boy, could they eat. Along with something akin to breakfast they added fried chicken and grits. Most of the servers who took orders knew what they wanted so they didn't have to explain it every time. They didn't talk too good. However, they could smile, big broad smiles from sweet hearts, showing off rather brown teeth from chewin' tobacco and drinkin' gallons of sweet tea. They were very pleasant persons and once ya got to know them you were a friend for life. You would be a particular friend if you knew and liked their mama, now dead, parked in the Agony Angel Cemetery five miles down the road. Their papa was in another place, outta town, the Notable Nursing Home. He had been there for years and wasn't sure just who he was. Never recognized Eric or Eddie and if he tried he mixed them up.

Well, folks were coming and going, regulars and visitors. Astra Fisic? Nope. No word, no phone call, nor text. Late. Not there.

The newspaper delivery person brought a whole new stack to the failing paper machine. Just try and get your quarters out if they git stuck! Not easy. Well he was supposed to change them on Saturdays but he usually forgot and the biggest crowd wanting one each would be Sunday morning. He put about 50 copies in the machine, retrieved the coins and left in his sleek black shiny Ford F-150. Whiplash wiggled out of the booth, quarters in hand, and went outside. Ugh, more thick, humid air. She gently put the money in the box and got out a fresh new paper. Hers did not git stuck. People just ought to be more careful, not in such a hurry (like I usually am!). She waddled back into Thee Café, trying not to trip on the rubber rug, and sank into the bench of the booth and began to read aloud under her breath.

Sarahfinna was interested but Melodious was still on the blues trail with BB King or Elvis.

"What's the headline?" Sarahfinna asked.

"Not sure all the type is the same size. But lookie here, a photo of that girls club going on a shopping trip. Says they went to a mall and to some big box stores and had a great time. Look there's Janney Wilson and Linda Lynn. No kidding, there's Astra Fisic in her red hat. I didn't know she liked to go shopping?"

"Naw, she doesn't but these girls do and she loves being with them! Wish she'd git here, I'm beginning to starve!" Slow down, Whiplash!

"Here's an article about the Castle HS teens and their robots. I am so impressed with them. Last year they did rockets and they did well. I mean we're only a small town and those kids had to compete with big high schools region-wide. To come fourteenth out of 60 in the state is pretty good! Go Team!" They high-fived each other as if they were still teens in high school themselves. Melodious didn't move.

++

Astra Fisic, yes, that's really my name. Yes, I regularly wear my favorite red hat. Well, yesterday I was sitting in the park, on a bench, eating my taco-free tacos and humming a tune I learned many years ago. I was not planning to visit with anyone and I had not made plans for anyone to come to the park with me. I was quite happy alone and it was a beautiful day. Today I am supposed to meet with Whiplash, Melodious and Sarahfinna at Thee Café. That always provides enough conversation for the week!

But yesterday the novel I was reading was engaging and I just kept going no matter how many folks walked or skated by. I was absorbed in the novel, not in the people. The sun was hot, though it would grow hotter as summer progressed here in the South. Lots of folks spoke... like, hey, or howdy, or afternoon. I had to raise my head, from my novel each time, and acknowledge them. Rarely was it someone I knew. That's why I came to this park and not the other one over by Thee Café. Didn't wanna chat. Good Southern manners? No? Often I lost my place. Curious, how that made me edgy and cross. I mean not a big deal really. Each time I thought if I just put my finger near the spot there would be no difficulty. But no, each greeting surprised me and I lost my place. Might have been better to read something less engrossing like the local paper, or one of my stargazer picture books.

Behind my bench was a large oak tree. I suspect it had been there many, many years. Sturdy and full and the ground showed off its reproductive potential with many, many acorns. One had to wonder, though, there were rarely any more trees growing from these hundreds of acorns. Didn't seem right, all that life, and nothing to show for it!

The bench was painted an off orange with a bit of rust trim. Rather attractive and if one looked across the park green they stood out clearly. There were maybe fifteen or twenty and nearly all had at least one sitter if not two. Off to my left was a young woman and an infant, oh, what, six, eight months old? The smiling child gurgled and cooed and the smiling mother was as enchanted with her as I was with my novel. We paid no attention to one another.

I finished my taco-free taco, washed up with one of those wet-wipes (the odor was repellent even for mosquitos, I'm sure) and drank my sugar-caffeine- and gluten free drink. A rather disgusting drink but quenched my thirst. The garbage can was a small walk off so I decided to put my waste in there and choose another bench for the rest of the afternoon.

That was yesterday. Well, some of it.

Today is Sunday and I am running late for my weekly with S., M. & W. this sounds a bit odd perhaps, but Saturdays I go to the park, if not heaving with rain. It is my day to decide on my 'random act of kindness.' Know what I mean? One tries to do a good deed without the person knowing who did it. Not exactly a game, but a way not to focus on myself but on another person. Say, if I went and got a burger and fries and delivered them to Gregory Gordon's apartment. He never gets out, loves fresh burgers, and he would not know it was me! Random act of kindness. I get no credit. I like that. Another way is to get in the drive-in-burger-line and pay for the burger or cuppa coffee of the person behind you…and then keep going.

I hadn't exactly decided on what I was going to do when the young woman and child approached me. She introduced herself simply as Percy and the little girl-child as Nevaeh (*ni-vey*). I guess this was around noon or 1pm. Anyway, we sat on another bench entirely away from the ones we had already frequented, and she began telling me of her situation. Percy was fifteen, Nevaeh was seven months. Work out the math. Once

7

I heard the story, however, I was so surprised and compelled to act. The acts of kindness would not be random they would be very specific.

++

Last year Percy was living with her mother in a tiny town in Georgia. Her uncle was a brash and hurtful man and one day her mom was showing that she was PG. Caftan was a sweet woman but had been told not to get PG again as it might cost her her life. Her uncle would not have been a suitable partner anyway! He hurt her so much. He should not have done that to her.

Well, long story short, Caftan went in her fifth month to an abortionist and died during the procedure. The infant, however, lived. Percy had gone with her mother, and at fifteen came out with a very fragile newborn sister. She named her Nevaeh and took her to the clinic near her home. Percy had many challenges, and she moved away from that house to a high school girlfriend's and the baby grew. The hospital unit had released her to Percy, all organs functioning very well, and they just hit the road. She wasn't sure where they were going but she knew it had to be far away from there. She had buried her mother in peace. The rickety old bus became their travel of choice and she came further south.

++

Well, you know the part about meeting in the park. Moving on.

++

Astra Fisic decided to be of some help to Percy. They went to eat and feed and change the baby girl. Nevaeh was a sweet tempered child and loved to laugh, great big giggles, right out-loud.

"I have an idea," Astra Fisic told Percy. I don't know if it will work out forever or if you would even be interested; it goes like this. My friend Beatrice lives on the other side of town. She has a pit bull named

SweetSue and a huge old four bedroom house. I thought we might go visit her. You and Nevaeh might just find a stopping place there for a while. Whaddya think?"

Percy wasn't too chatty, very tired, and sorta scared. She nodded her head and looked down at Nevaeh who was smiling, smiling. It made her smile as well.

They set out from the park and arrived at Astra Fisic's car. She called Beatrice and briefly explained the situation. They were welcome to come. On the way they did some shopping for the baby, for Percy, for food, and a surprise for Beatrice and SweetSue.

After they arrived and chatted a little, Beatrice showed Percy to a very large bedroom with an attached bath. There was a wonderful white crib in the corner, near a dressing table full of diapers and wonderful smelling lotions. The crib had a quilt in it and some tiny sheets with a little pillow. There was a corner all fitted-out with toys and a little rug with building blocks printed on it. There were numbers and letters and a very sweet doll.

"Well, whaddya think?" Beatrice asked.

"Yes, ma'am, thissel be perfect for me'n ma suster. Thanks you too much, bless your heart!"

Around and down a couple of halls, following their noses they ended up in the dining room. Dinner disappeared. Beatrice fell for Nevaeh and Percy. They fell for her. Unless something went very wrong indeed, this might be a forever home for the two happy sisters. And it was right on the high school bus line for Percy.

++

"I know I'm over an hour late," said Astra, a little out of breath, trying to apologize as Sarahfinna, Melodious and Whiplash grumped at her.

"We had to eat, you know."

9

"Yes, yes, no problem" she assured them. "I am so sorry but if you want to know why and what happened we could sit down for a little while and I'll tell you about Nevaeh and Percy." Astra Fisic hoped they would, but they were still grumping on her. They had their reasons clearly.

"You couldda phoned."

"Yes, I would 'uv if I wasn't dead asleep. And the phone was off, if you hadda tried to phone me! I am super sorry."

They looked back and forth at one another and then smiled and agreed to sit for a minute for Astra Fisic, in her red hat, was there for Sunday morning breakfast and they needed to hear her story and she needed to eat, bless her heart!

"Well, yesterday, I was in the park reading my novel…"

THE END

Astra Fisic and the Quilt With No Particular Pattern

Astra Fisic had taken up a new hobby, quilting. Her three grumpy friends Whiplash, Melodious and Sarahfinna were not interested in quilting at all; at least not in the beginning. They only enjoyed breakfast at Thee Café on Sundays and other activities during the week.

Astra, however, had other plans. She wanted classes, she bought the magazines, and she even had a whole set of *PBS* DVDs about the history of quilting. Astra Fisic was a slightly retired astronomer and she had a friend Alcor who was trying to become an author. One thing she did very well was paint. She was not interested in quilting either. Or so she said, not at this time!

So Astra Fisic set out to learn everything she could about quilting, from the most basic to perhaps something a little complicated like those big *American Stars*. Her first trip was onto the internet where she discovered U TUBE and patterns, stores for shopping, and how she could make a quilt all on her own. She and her friend Beatrice had discussed making one for Nevaeh, that's Percy's baby sister, but cancelled that plan for later. What Astra Fisic wanted to do was go to the fabric shop on the uptown downtown-only-one-in-town Main Street. Everyone in town called the owner, designer, teacher, and beautiful woman, Ms. Super-Craft (mostly referred to, however, as Ms. C.). She always helped everyone who came in and was cheerful and thoughtful. If you could explain your project to her, she often had very good and clever suggestions. Astra went to visit the *FABULOUS FABRIC SHOPPE*.

It was a bit like going into a church, thought Astra, when she opened the door the little bell rang, and she was quickly surrounded by bolts and bolts of wonderful fabric, like stained glass windows in the silence. Astra tiptoed. So still. Hushed. Happy. As she stood there and began to take in the beauty, a few voices, and then laughter, and then a 'hey, hi, whaddya need?' came flying over the baskets full of embroidery thread.

"Just lookin' for now," she sent back. "Will need your help in a minute."

"OK, enjoy and just let me know!" Ms. C. sang back.

Astra began handling the materials. Some were soft and others very fleecy. Some were very thin, like silk and others were coarse and hard like canvas. Amazing, she thought, the makers of material. The colors so rich and the endless possibilities of what might be made, worn, or used to adorn a table or put on a wall. And then there were the special ones you crawled under for a cozy night's sleep! Little girls dresses and baby boys pants; bags and satchels, quilted and sewn were hanging here and there. The local Castle High School mascot and the neighboring universities colors were all available.

Astra heard a few voices coming from the back and there were some of her very whacky friends buying material too. The next quilting class was about to begin and they were getting ready. Ms. C. had room for 14 and she had almost filled the class Beatrice was going to teach for six weeks on Tuesdays and Thursdays from one until three in the afternoon. The A/C worked well in the classroom and it was perfect for summertime. With materials, it only cost $20.

Everyone turned around to greet Astra Fisic. Laughing, and 'hey' and 'howdy', and 'hi,' filled the classroom. 'Are ya gonna join us?' bounced off the walls and into Astra's ears. "Well, why not?" she said with great joy. "Why not? You are some of my very weirdest friends and if we all learn to quilt together maybe one day we can make <u>one</u> quilt together?"

"Well, now...." some mumbled, others seemed to like the idea, others were grumpy. You know why! Melodious, Sarahfinna and Whiplash were there.

Astra Fisic went around hugging folks and just feeling very happy inside to know that she would be meeting at Ms. C.'s *Shoppe* with all these wonderful women, twice the week. Oh my! That might be a lot! That might be too much! Hahahahahaha.

Have to tell you who was there, and funny thing though they all do not come every week, each one finished her little 9- patch block!

Meet Swampy, a dog trainer from Nawlins', ChaChalita, a dancer originally from Argentina, Effie who is 'one with nature', Gal raises horses, Roz has false teeth that fall out of place, and BobbyLou is a country music geek. At another table is Joyus who loves Christmas and drives her purple electric wheelie like a mad woman, Ducky who loves to swim in the local lake, Angel with her pink- powdered hair and Donut, usually eating a bit more than she should. Already mentioned are the three sisters. That makes thirteen...and Astra Fisic would be fourteen. "Oh, come on," they cheered her.

Astra being a bit shy really preferred to be alone, but saw their happy faces and could not resist. "OK why not? I'll get Ms. C. to help me choose my materials and I will see you next Tuesday!"

++

Astra took her material home and spread it out on her bed. One day, she thought, I'll make a quilt to fit my twin-bed. Today, however, I'm going to learn and will make me a 9-patch. She had chosen nine fat quarters, half in dark tones, and half in light. Some were reds and pinks and some were blues and stars. Of course, she'd have to have at least some stars, being a slightly retired astronomer. One of the fat quarters was a very bright yellow/gold with a luminous pattern of wavy lines. Looked like sun streaks. The other piece she loved was full of purple, fading in and out, as on a stormy night with clouds. This outta make a lovely wall decoration for my little workroom/studio, she thought. I cain't wait!! Carefully she folded the fat quarters and put them in the bag. Only four days till Tuesday.

++

Percy and Nevaeh decided to go to the walking-park and Beatrice dropped them off on her way shopping. "See youz guyz in an hour or so?"

"Yea, indeedy," chuckled Percy. Nevaeh waved and clutched her little fuzzy striped monkey even tighter.

They had become great friends and Percy was getting ready to return to high school in August, and Beatrice just loved having Nevaeh at home. Beatrice was the quilting class teacher, so Percy and Nevaeh could either come or not. Percy wasn't too interested in quilting but after some thought decided to make something small for Nevaeh.

++

Astra had some ideas even before she learned to quilt. She wanted to make lap blankets for the Notables Nursing Home or even those little bags to hang on walkers and Beatrice wanted to make something for the homeless. Maybe little packs or bags to carry some of their things in?

Nobody said you *had* to do for others but Sarahfinna wanted <u>for sure</u> to keep hers for herself. Having to give anything away caused her to be grumpy. Melodious' grumps came because the teacher, no matter what she was learning, tried to get her to follow the directions. She always knew what she was doing *was* right. In quilting this is very necessary skill. Things are cut, ironed, sewn together correctly or it's a wonky quilt. Whiplash had big grumps because she wanted hers done tomorrow, not in six weeks. She had no patience and can't remember why she agreed to do a quilt. They take forever to make. Let's just gitter done!

++

Tuesday morning came round and Astra Fisic finished her stargazing notes. There had been two shooting stars the previous night. Hadn't seen one for a while, she thought. Her binoculars were strong, almost better than her telescope, and she saw Saturn and Jupiter. Notes done, she packed away that gear and got out her little bag. Inside were the nine fat quarters, thread, pins, scissors (only for cutting cloth) and the three possible patterns, she hadn't made a decision yet. She put on her red hat and headed out. Lunch would be at Thee Café and she would eat the daily *red, white and blue plate.* Tuesdays were usually something like mac and cheese, baked chicken parts, and a fruit salad for desert. If they had sweet potatoes, she'd have a scoop. If not, cornbread. Water and ice would be enough to drink. $5 senior lunch. Lovely. At about 12:45pm she would begin to wander down to the *FABULOUS FABRIC SHOPPE* for her lesson.

++

Beatrice was ready with lots of teaching tools and beautiful materials. Her helper, Percy was there, and the wee one was asleep in her little carryall. Folks shuffled in and took seats at either a round or rectangular table.

Beatrice welcomed them all and after a little minute of silence to ask for focus and working well together, she began their first lesson. She was a great teacher and had brought with her a variety of finished quilts, batting, threads, measuring tools, cutting tools (including a circular cutter and board), wax paper, a hot iron, patterns, and by break time, everyone's interest was piqued.

After the break she asked each one a bit about her idea for her 9-patch. Some were so unfamiliar with quilting (or sewing) they didn't have any idea yet. Others who had done some were ready to cut and sew. Astra Fisic was about in the middle along with Swampy, ChaChalita, and Joyus. They had studied up a bit in the past week and with a little help would be able to get to work.

Beatrice got the ones going who knew something about what they were doing, talked to Astra Fisic and her little group and had them practice measuring and cutting on the bias (45degree angle to the selvages). The other little group needed one-to-one. It is a big class. Eventually some of these quilters would know enough to help each other.

++

Astra Fisic was a little tired when she returned home after the first lesson but in the subsequent weeks, she paced herself. It wasn't the quilting as much as the energy she spent with the women. She was such an introvert, and so many of them were extroverts. Each one was so beautiful and so different. She tried to quilt like everybody else and listened carefully to Beatrice's instructions. Some folks loved to laugh and chat, some had headsets on and others got their threads all tangled, and even others just sat and didn't work much. Never mind, thought Astra, I am going to learn and plug along. And that is what she did.

++

The lesson yesterday was about basting (putting in those very large temporary stitches) and batting (no, not like in baseball). The blocks were beautifully sewn to form each 9-patch top. When the top was finished, they needed batting and a back, and perhaps a border. Batting was old nylons, or plastic bags. It might be old socks or cotton strips from old clothes. Beatrice suggested all of those and everyone just laughed. Then she produced big bags of white cotton fuzzy stuff... looked a bit like cotton balls but flattened out into sheets.

"The thicker your batting is," she told them, "the warmer the quilt. If you are doing a table runner or a wall decoration, you only need enough to give form to your top. If you intend to sleep under it...well..." We shifted in our chairs. "Once your top is done and sewn to the back and the batting is in...*then* you quilt! Quilting is a variety of very tiny stiches (if done by hand) making its own pattern. You may also machine stitch, setting your pattern for whatever designs you desire." She showed us some examples. They were just stunning.

++

About four weeks through the lessons, Angel and ChaChalita proposed an idea to the group. They had shared the same table for all the lessons, and knew each other from previous town activities. Angel gently pushed back a swatch of pink-powdered hair and asked, "Do y'all think we could, well, could we, maybe we'd like to..." and couldn't quite get it all out. She looked over at ChaChalita who picked up with, "yes, we wondered if our muy mucho maravillosa colcha pieces might not get connected into a big grande quilt to be somewhere others peoples can see we did it like togethers?"

There were *hum's* and *aha's* now that the women had progressed pretty far and had come to like their work very much. Astra Fisic looked over to Beatrice who was working with Gal and Roz. They didn't speak but smiled, wanting the other women to give their opinions first.

"Well, I can tell you right now," (Guess who? Yup!) Sarahfinna said, "I'm takin' mine home to live in my kitchen."

Donut indicated she would be willing to put hers with the others. Swampy and Effie were also willing. BobbyLou was reluctant because she had had such a hard time doing it. Ducky, Gal, and Joyus were as cheerful as they could be. "Yes, yes, yes," and that was that. Melodious and Whiplash were none too happy but grumpily agreed to be a part of the maravillosa colcha. Let's see that was nine. Astra Fisic agreed and so did Angel. Was that everyone?

Ah, no, Roz said, "*nooo* way. This is going home with me! I want it for myself just to prove I did it!" ChaChalita looked as if she was going to cry when Roz said that, but she was very happy to put hers in. All these were almost quilted and each woman was so proud of her 9-patch block. Now they had twelve and the colcha could be sewn together when they were all done.

Beatrice explained the next stages. The twelve 9- patches would be laid out and arranged. What a wonderful big top for a quilt! Now Beatrice had to help them sew the whole thing together. Somebody (ies) had to pick out material for the border. One very large piece of material had to be chosen for the back (unless they decided to just stitch all the tops together using their own backs). When all that was done they needed a *hanging sleeve* at the top on the back to slide a dowel through. Ready to install. It would only be finished though after every quilter signed and dated her block. Oh my, finishing touches also took time (or so Whiplash grumpily pointed out!).

++

A bit of cooing and a little cry came from Nevaeh and all the quilters began to pay attention to her (the grumpies, a little less). Percy had made a lovely little quilted bag for her pacifier, along with one or two other things. She was changed, passed around after powdering, lotioning and feeding. She didn't need clean clothes but Joyus changed her outfit anyway. Angel combed what hair she had and Gal put on her little boots. Now all she needed was a horse! Nevaeh laughed, gurgled, and took the tickling and precious smiles from all her 'aunties' with grace and charm.

++

This colcha wasn't going to be a 'Crazy Quilt', it was going to be a quilt with no particular pattern. A pattern repeats itself and within the 9-patches there were certainly patterns. But all together, no.

Here are the patterns the *Only-One-In-Town-Quilt-Club* women stitched: Crosshatch Block, Row Houses Block, Rail Fence, Winter Migration, Gray Unicorn, Rainbow Heart, Star Flower, Magic Pinwheel, Rolling Square, Scrappy Strips, Snail's Trail, Triple Square, Buzzsaw Block and Whirligig Garden (that was Astra's). Put those altogether and what do you have? A quilt with no particular pattern! These, among thousands of others are known all over the quilt world. Some are more difficult than others some take longer to do. Color, too, can form patterns. Beatrice had helped each quilter pick out her material and pattern making it possible for each unique work.

Equally, the quilter can design a block and then repeat it. Look at the amazing quilts from Gees Bend women, using real-old materials left over from making their children's clothing. Odd bits of jeans, and then stripes and strips of someone's old dress forms most simple but eye-catching patterns. These are such amazing works of art, some are installed in the Smithsonian.

The only pattern this quilt exhibits is *persons*...yes, women-type-persons. They are the only repeating pattern. They come twice a week. They stich and quilt. They laugh and discuss. Over and over. It remains, however, a quilt (colcha) with no particular pattern and is installed in the County Court House hallway near the bench.

The clerk looks at it every day and says he never gets tired of it. The judge comes in and looks at a different part each time. Purple was her favorite color. And the children from the school get up real close and touch it! Yes, touch it (it's OK) and feel the different materials. They went back one time to their school and made a quilt out of paper squares, and decorated their classroom.

++

Oh, and it was Beatrice, Melodious, and BobbyLou who chose the material for the border. Donut and Ducky picked out the material for the back. Beatrice, Percy and Astra did some of the sewing it all together, along with Swampy and ChaChalita. Whiplash, Gal and Angel made sure the hanging sleeve was ready to go, with a strong, long dowel.

Don't be unhappy that Roz and Sarahfinna weren't a part of that project. Maybe they needed to have their 9-patch at home? Maybe they will share in next one. Next one? Why yes. In only three weeks, the intermediate quilting lessons would begin. Wonder who will show? Maybe Astra Fisic in her bright red hat?

THE END

3

Astra Fisic and the Painters
of the Summer Sky

or…maybe my friend Astra Fisic, the lady in the red hat, can help?

Alcor (named after the constellation) closed her journal and stared out the window as a misty fog arose from the pond. I do get sick of writing such dribble, she thought. Maybe I need to paint more and write less? A Canadian goose flew low over the pond followed by another and another and another all honking. Gorgeous, strong, and good eating… leaving behind lots of poop.

OK, OK, I'm moving.

She lifted her stiff legs off the couch and headed for the shower. Only an hour until she needed to show. Can't I stay home and write or paint? NO, because each time I do that I eat or watch TV or find something else to do besides write and I go broke and feel broken. NO, I have to make a living and stacking cans or working in the freezer at the *GROCER'S PICKS* in my tiny town, Castle, MS, is my way to stay independent.

Everything is ordinary, always the same…even to being the same moans and worries, the same difficulties and differences. Boring! It's always the same people, the same post office and the same thrift shop. The same little Thee Café and the same police. The library, a favorite place of refuge, is peaceful and cool in the long, hot MS summers. Lots to read, watch or hear. Silence mostly and a peace that comes over me so that I can think, reflect and read the great novels of others, always hoping to write my own. Usually it's closed, though, by the time I get off work and not open on Saturdays.

OK, OK I'm going.

Alcor picked up her little pack with lunch and meds and headed for the truck. Winding down the hill, through the woods into town, she watched carefully as the gravel crunched beneath the truck tires. The dust flew behind and she wondered how many dings would fill the front windshield. None yesterday- a miracle. She parked the truck as far away as she could get and then walked briskly toward the automatically opening doors of *GP*, where she saw the same people on her shift, smelled the same grocery smells, and was refreshed by the cool air.

Mr. Jason P. Kilwisden, owner, is standing at the till awaiting her arrival. 8:00AM sharp. He is there at the beginning of every shift, making sure they are on time, properly dressed, and alert. He nods, looks at his watch, looks up at her, and gives that tiny smile that makes his mustache quiver. She was free to begin work.

Alcor wandered back to the so-called staff lounge. Really, it was only a closet with her one hook among many (like in kindergarten only taller) where she could hang her bag and jacket in trade for her official *GP* apron. She slipped it over her head and hooked the belt behind her. The pocket still contained her week's work list and she turned it to Tuesday, where she would work in the freezer, chopping and arranging the meats and cheeses. Five packaged picks for $19.99. What a bargain. Polish sausage, rib-eyes, hamburger, chicken (thighs, breasts, or wings), others you could mix and match. When she finished this shift her hands would ache like crazy, but, it was only once a week in the freezer, not worth trying to find another job. There weren't any anyway. *GP* was the only store in town.

There was no festive or background music at *GP*. She never knew why and there would be no complaints. Why not the local Gospel station played at the hairdressers, or the gas station? No, just the sounds of jostling carts, and the cleavers cutting through the meat or cheese, hitting the boards beneath. The swishing sound of saran wrap. Snap! Tightly affixing to each, package after package and the clicks of the little scale weighing the contents, spitting out the printed label for sticking on neatly in the upper right hand corner. A child crying (or even screaming on occasion), the low hushed voices of people greeting one another out in the store proper away from her freezer where no one spoke.

No one paid any attention to anyone else until break time, almost three hours into the eight-hour shift. Alcor's quota for the time from beginning to first break was twenty packages. Might be the meats, the cheeses, or both depending on need, and the plan of her twenty-eight or something year old supervisor, Rhyonda. There were three on each shift in the freezer/meat department. Alcor, and either Timmy or Ralph, and Rhyonda. They got on well. Knew their jobs. Never spoke, focused on work and waited for the break.

That day it was Ralph. At break, he bolted for the 'lounge' door, went to get his diet *DR PEPPER* and headed out of the building for his truck. The break was exactly fifteen minutes, just enough time for his drink and to warm himself in the over 100degrees front seat of his old '79 green Ford pick-up, with very high and large tires, yet sporting an antique tag. He looked down at his watch. The face had fogged up and he could not see the time. He did not want to return too early and certainly not late for Mr. Kilwisden would be watching. Ralph had only worked at *GP* for less than a year and still wondered about Mr.

Kilwisden and what he actually *did* besides watch the staff, insuring they were always on time and tidy.

Ralph stretched out behind the wheel and stared out the window. His job was a real drag. I mean I went to college for two years and got an AA degree, he mused as rock-a-billy music played on his MP3. What good did it do me? Here I am freezing to death once a week and not doing much more the rest of the week. $8.92 an hour- barely minimum wage. It doesn't take much, however, to do what I do. His thoughts moved to more money, with less responsibility...how can I *own* a store?

As a youngster, he had never been very aggressive or assertive for that matter. He did OK 'C's/B's' in HS was voted *Best Personality* when he graduated in 1992. He stayed out of school for a year or so and then went to the local (55 miles away) community college for two years majoring in life, girls, a little drinking, and even business administration and local history. He graduated in 1997 and set out to change the world.

A man of very few principles he had gathered from an occasionally-around father and a non-interactive mother. If he could get it done, earned, or stolen '*easy*', that was his plan.

Alcor saw the man approach Ralph's truck and knock on his window. She had never seen him before and there were rarely true strangers in town. Often folks only came in monthly or at best twice a month if it included a haircut or perm. But they would be recognized by someone and most here at the *GP*. The next thing she saw was the man getting into the passenger side of the truck and they drove off together like a shot. There were only eight minutes left of the break. Wherever he had gone, he'd not be back on time.

The man looked ordinary enough, jeans and trainers with a light, white shirt hanging out. It was already over 102degrees. He had moved slowly and did not seem agitated. His summer cowboy hat in hand and reflective sunglasses around his neck made him look like just about every other guy around who was mid-late 20's. They turned left out of the parking lot squealing tires and she watched until she could see the rear of the pick-up no longer. Curious. She headed back to the lounge for her final five or so minutes.

++

68 packages today, she jotted in her journal. Alcor sat on her bed, looking out the window at the trees that grew up around her place. *I really wonder where Ralph went the other day. He has become so secretive, it's like I don't know him anymore. We did, after all go to school together many years ago.* She closed her journal.

++

The MS sun was high in the sky already sizzling by 8am and the day would swelter on. Drips and drops of perspiration from every conceivable spot on the body absorbed by the lightest of clothing, and quickly discharged for shorter and skimpier ones after work. It was those days she preferred the freezer…when she got off at 3:30pm. This week she had to work Saturday morning as well. It rotated, like everything else, all's fair, Mr. Kilwisden, always said. But things weren't really fair, she thought. Just look around, or read the papers, listen to the news. Things are not the least bit fair. Alcor felt resigned and that sinking feeling filled her stomach, gurgled a bit, and then she got on to something else.

She drove her truck away from the *GP* up through an area badly destroyed some weeks before by an F4 tornado, fires still burning, backhoes and small diggers removing stumps, people still out collecting things from the trees and raking up. It was amazing how some houses and trees stood their ground and all the massive trees surrounding them were devastated … new roofs gleamed in the sun; latest fashion metal in green, red, or gold.

Some roads were rough, still gravel or badly paved with only one or two thin coats of tar. Other roads and streets were beautiful... clear lines, smooth stretches, holes filled in. For miles and miles there were trees of many flavors. Pine plantations had filled the area and hardwoods sacrificed for a quicker harvest. Where the hardwoods had brought more income they took longer, maybe thirty years before cutting, compared to the pine -harvestable in twelve to fourteen years. Most farmers had had to diversify anyway...could not live on cattle or cotton alone anymore so if they had the land, they planted pines, obtained free from the agricultural department (when they had them).

++

The evening came, a long evening as the sun never seemed to set...just filled the sky with deep purples, oranges and a little wisp of white from the few clouds that were dispersing. Bright, shining, almost blazing behind, was what was left of the sun's flaming face. Will she arise tomorrow? Is this the last night of the world? Alcor had stopped her truck at a favorite overlook, scanning afar the valley filled with trees and trees and trees all tinted with orange, glowing in the last vestiges of the day now gone.

++

Soon the stars of the summer sky would be out and everywhere one looked would be stars twinkling and bright shining planets, especially Saturn and Jupiter. The summer triangle of Vega, Deneb and Altair, though not as bright as Venus, a buff like Alcor could easily see. She knew her stars. She loved her planets. Jupiter had four prominent moons (69 in all) and Saturn's rings were clear and awesome. Sometimes one might even see her moons. And from way over in Perseus would soon be coming the Perseid Meteor shower @ fifteen an hour for a few hours. *Awwesoome*, awesome, Alcor thought. Have to stay up late for those, though. Never mind, work came around and she would be off. Nothing entertained nor developed her imagination though, as the night sky.

Alcor might have become an astronomer if anyone knew how much she loved the stars. But no one knew. Her college program only had introductory courses, those she did take, but they were not enough to get into an upper college program. Alcor was not particularly good at math and that proved somewhat of a difficulty. Her other sciences, especially geology, were OK but astronomy, now that was the best! So she studies with Astra Fisic, a slightly retired astronomer. There seemed to be nothing she didn't know about the stars and planets. Alcor really looked up to her and wanted to keep learning!

Taking out her portable clip-on light, Alcor read in her Journal and then began to write:

> *I read a novel last week that stole my heart, SMOKE JUMPERS by Evans. How did he move from one continent to another, one culture to another, always intertwining the characters, from such a simple start, a tiny beginning? Maybe only two or three main ideas: relationships, jobs and adventures; is it really just that simple? Three characters who live out interesting twists in their lives and how that bears out upon one another; who hold certain jobs, change jobs, and share jobs, through a series of quite amazing adventures. Seems anyone could do that. Yet maybe I should be painting again, photography, anything but writing!*

Sure enough, the sun arose, earlier and earlier, hotter and hotter, and she got up, showered and ate a bit of breakfast. Already muggy.

She had changed her eating habits recently, mostly eating some kind of fruit and perhaps a piece of Jewish rye with fig preserve, a granola she could chew, or 9-grain toast. Water or chamomile tea fit the bill. She took her snack to work and had it at first break. The rising sun filled the window on her enclosed porch. Her old grey wicker rocker was her favorite place to pray and sit silently allowing the freshness of the new day to fill her. It was Alcor's place to say thank you to her Creator, though, she was not much of a 'church person' she was working on it.

The night before, the moon had been a large distinct orange ball. It was low in the sky and the moisture, dust and smoke caused the orange color. The higher in the sky the whiter, with that 'old –man- face' made very clear.

There had been a cat of some kind hanging around her place. She wasn't a 'cat-person'…appreciated their color, ingenuity, and skill…but sneezes followed petting etc., so she looked from afar. She could tell there had been a cat partly because the birds were nervous and the two dogs that patrolled her road were skittish. Perhaps the cat was feral or thrown away, like so many kittens and puppies, with the trash.

Unlike her neighbors who filled bird feeders, Alcor threw birdseed out each day and let the birds look for seeds by themselves. Very little fighting that way and because she loved watching them she made sure there was a good mixture of seeds. Last year she had hung up nectar for the hummingbirds that flew in on their way further south…but not this year.

This year she fed the birds, and added two fish and a turtle to her circle. Ivory was a black molly and Hiccup was a little stripy neon thing. Anyway, they seemed to get along as they swam in a good friend's grandmother's beautiful clear 'sugar jar'. The friend was over 80…so the bowl must have been well over 125 years! She had almost run over the turtle in the road a few weeks back and decided to get out and bring it home (not generally a good policy!). Turtle was wounded by someone else and would likely be a snack for a predator. Alcor suspected it was a 'she'…not very long fingernails. It was a three-toed box turtle and there were plenty of worms still for sale as the fishing season peaked. Turtle loved to take the wiggly worm from her fingers…though she had to watch out…that little girl had a snap! Eventually Alcor named her Mizar.

Ouch, time for work.

++

If you looked for things to watch or new things in town, one might look at the remains of the railroad's railcars. Alcor really liked watching the little crews on the rails scrubbing and then re-painting them in their bright blue company uniform. She even tried to get a job there once. Summer was not a good time to be employed by the *MS & TN* in and out of those large cars. Hot, hot, very hot indeed.

There were very stylized paintings on the cars from some big city spray-painter and they stood out. Reds and blues, black and of course, white stood out on the sky blue background. Words she did not always understand were block printed or written in a sort of calligraphy. Must say, Alcor thought, they are surely big enough spaces for great murals and words. I would so like to paint a mural on just one car, maybe get some of the neighbors to help out, maybe something of the history of the town or county? They seem to leave behind a car or two that don't get moved for weeks. Sometimes there's even a FOR SALE sign nearby. We could do it in that space of time if we knew what we were doing and if we had the paints and other equipment all in place! Maybe we could paint the summer sky?

++

Or the winter sky or anything but work in this freezer, Alcor thought. Maybe we could include 'star-baby' of the Aboriginal people's creation story? Or Baby-Jesus from ours. Why I could just continue thinking up so many stories we could paint on just one car…both sides, of course!

Ralph got back (only two minutes late and that was acceptable for an emergency) and was quietly working next to Alcor, slicing up chicken breasts for packaging. Alcor continued to package hoop cheese and polish sausage. Her goal was twenty-two packs of each before quitting time.

++

Alcor had a day-off coming and she decided to go to the planetarium, in the capitol past Nearby City. Check with Astra Fisic... she might just come along. The summer sky was the program and as she had been thinking so much about how to get a railcar she could paint, she needed to do some sketching in her book. No better place than the planetarium.

She headed out early as it was about a two hour drive. Her little truck putted along nicely and it was a glorious day. Alcor had not been to the planetarium for a long time. The last show she saw was the winter sky and the previous one was something about the moon. As she approached the parking lot she saw Astra Fisic standing there awaiting her.

++

Here's how things can take a 180degree shift. Astra Fisic, a slightly retired astronomer, who almost always wears a red hat, met Alcor in the parking lot and they proceeded into the screening of the *SUMMER SKY*. It was so well done. Despite the many times Astra Fisic had seen similar, she always marveled at the vast creativity of the Creator! Alcor too, was stunned by the beauty. When they left, they settled on walking a few blocks until they found a little restaurant and decided to have bite of lunch, late though it was. Their conversation went back and forth about the sky and the planets and Astra Fisic's new project.

++

Astra Fisic had done many things in her life but she was famous for being an astronomer. She had studied in college, of course, but she was one of those people who liked to study on her own and so she knew many things beyond her academics. Her experience took her far and wide to various countries, to see their telescopes and astronomical equipment. She referred to herself as 'slightly' retired because she wanted to keep her hand in it. Astra Fisic loved giving little lectures on this or that and particularly loved teaching the smaller children about the heavens, her favorite reference.

"Howz things in the freezer?" she quipped.

Alcor felt a big smile forming on her face. "My-tee chilly!"

"Ya still liken' it?"

"Ah, never did but gotta makka few bucks."

"Well, I havva new project and I want you to be a part of it. If I paid you the same as yer makin' jest now…howz 'bout it?"

Alcor was shocked. Her role model, the woman she really looked up to, and wanted to imitate…had just asked her to come to work. "Well, I, I, I," she stammered, "I gotta…"

"You gotta what?"

"Well, I…I guess I'm just so knocked out I don't know what to say. Can you tell me more about your project?"

"Ah, no, 'cauze it's jest beginnin' and I'm not sure of all the moving parts. Would that matter a lot?"

"Well, no, you've already said you'd pay me…that's the rent and stuff. Well, why not? I was just thinkin' on a new project myself!"

"Whaddya have in mind?"

"Naw, never mind, just a little dream I guess. Anyway I want to be involved with your project and we'll jest have to see how much time is available fer mine."

So they didn't even give each other hints as to what they were thinkin' 'bout. Well, not for a week or two. Alcor left Mr. Kilwisden and the *GP* freezer and reported to work on the first of the month. She never found out what Ralph was up to but her sights were set much higher now…right to the heavens.

++

They met at Astra Fisic's favorite place, Thee Café for breakfast, not Sunday. Sunday was the day she met her friends (the three grumpy sisters, Whiplash, Melodious and Sarahfinna). No, it was Thursday and available was the *red-white-and blue plate*. Thursday was coleslaw, pork chops and black-eyed peas and/or butter beans. They also had cornbread, and blueberry cobbler. However, since it was breakfast they ate tall-stacks, scrambled eggs, and very crispy bacon. Astra Fisic drank de-café coffee. They never had any so she brought her own. Alcor had coke. Regular coke with lottsa ice.

++

The following Tuesday morning was full of surprises for both Astra Fisic and Alcor. They had their first (and perhaps only) business meeting. Astra Fisic started.

"Well, I want to paint the skies, the heavens, the story of Creation somewhere so the people in our town and county will appreciate the story in the Scriptures."

"You wanna do what?" Alcor was flummoxed. She could not believe what she had just heard.

"Well, I want the Creation story of the heavens and the earth to become a beauty spot in our town and I cain't figggure out where or how or when."

"Really?" Alcor hung in there.

"You? Any ideas?"

"Weell, you'll hardly believe this but *my* project idea I wouldn't tell you about is sorta like this. I wanted to paint the summer sky on one side and the winter sky on the other of an old railcar parked over by the disused warehouse."

"Really? Well, I know I hired you because you could design and paint, but I had no idea you were dreamin' on this! I think we're onto something big! What else?"

"Well, when the big blue *MS&TN* comes through here the guys are hired to clean up the cars from all the spray painting so they can go back into the fleet. Sometimes they have a railcar for sale. I was hoping to save enough money to buy a railcar, get them to move it into a more prominent place, get some folks from town to participate and then..."

"Yea! We can all git into it!"

They sat there and continued to laugh and plan. Astra Fisic was willing to find the money for the railcar. Alcor was to begin some sketches of the creation of the skies...the darkness and the light, the lights in the dome, the sun and the moon, the stars, and..."

"Listen, figggure this," Astra Fisic quizzed her young friend. "On the first day, 'light was created' BUT it wasn't until the fourth day we git sun, moon, and stars!" (Gen 1:1-19)

"Hadn't thought of that but will make my sketches more interesting."

++

The project was clearly underway. About a month later they came back to Thee Café on a Wednesday, fried chicken, spuds, creamed corn, and fruit salad (cornbread and/or blueberry cobbler). Alcor had her sketchbook full of ideas and they looked through pages and pages. Some were just drawings, some had words from Scripture and others were just ideas. Astra Fisic loved what she saw. She had done some of her homework as well. She was still waiting for the railcar price, but found a railcar just to her liking.

"I've thought of something else."

Alcor looked over at her with a inquiring smile. "What?"

"Well, I think we'll turn the inside of the railcar into a science center. Whaddya think?"

Alcor could do nothing but agree. "How cool is that? Maybe we can get some of the local teachers to help?"

"Just my thought," she said, as she swallowed a bite of fried chicken. "What do you think about painting the summer/winter sky as well?"

"I think it would be *fabulllouss*! Work those star formations into your designs and then let us look again in a week or two. Perhaps I'll have more information as well."

++

Over the next few months Astra Fisic and Alcor designed and worked on their project...making it an *'our'* project by involving folks from the town and county. They worked well together, and Astra Fisic was even able to get Melodious, Whiplash and Sarahfinna involved with the painting and the cleaning out of the insides and the beginnings of the science classrooms...one for astronomy and one for general inter-active science study. They hardly ever complained because they were so tired. Equally, they were very happy to be working with Astra Fisic and they almost always talked about the progress of the project on Sundays at Thee Café. Alcor had been invited to join them. She always had her sketchbook with her. Astra Fisic had a small spiral notebook, just in case they thought of some idea that needed to be noted. They ate and talked.

++

Astra Fisic decided to have a small inventory one morning. Why, they had desks, chairs and tables, glass cases for displays, globes and even a telescope (that occasionally worked). Astra Fisic set it up so that it pointed to prominent places. On hand were some binoculars and a couple of hunters donated scopes from their old guns. For the other classroom, there were magnifying glasses, bug-boxes, posters and drawing paper. She found colors and ink pens, rulers and scissors and even pots to be painted, and grass to be grown. All these things were donations from neighbors all over the place. A prize piece, however, was the railroad clock, built locally many years ago. It would find pride of place in the science center and would remind all Astra and Alcor's friends of the beauty of time well spent in creative pursuits and the regularity of sun and moon, stars and planets.

++

The project took many months. Some of the setbacks were due to weather or sickness, or even just downright tiredness. Students had to go back to school so painting on the outside was slower. Neither Alcor nor Astra Fisic worried though as they had lot of community relations work to do. Astra Fisic was frequently in the elementary and middle schools to do teaching and little workshops. This made her very happy because all the things she 'knew' she could share. The teachers were very happy as well.

Alcor was invited to be an assistant teacher in the small Castle High School art department. That had been Percy's idea. She was able to help the students in a variety of art styles and encouraged them to '*work outside the box*' (her secret code for 'help paint the railcar'!)

++

On a Monday at Thee Café, the *red-white & blue plate* was hamburger steak with brown gravy, mashed potatoes, coleslaw, corn on the cob, and a scoop of mac 'n cheese. Astra Fisic, Alcor, the three *grumpies*, the Mayor and the President of the county board gathered for lunch. They would be the first little planning committee for the Opening of *THE DOGWOOD STARS SCIENCE CENTER*. It was almost a year since the project had begun. Finances and donations were discussed. What was still needed was discussed. Dates and times were discussed. Guest speaker(s) was discussed. Why they'd even invite the new Governor. Parking and fees were discussed though the Opening would be free of charge. They agreed to meet each Monday until they felt they were ready to go.

++

Three weeks later at the hall. About 150 people came, including the planning committee. Again, the question of when the Opening would be arose high on the agenda.

The date suggested for the Opening was: August 21. Astra Fisic looked at them like they were nuts.

"We cain't have it that day…why there's to be a total eclipse of the sun! and I gotta go to Nashville to see it!" Folks *oooooed* and *ahhhed* and laughed and clapped.

As she said it, of course, they remembered.

"So when then?" the Mayor asked? "So when then?" the board President asked. "We've got calendars to keep and we need to be sure all the people can come!"

"When?"

"How about a Saturday? That way all the kids are out of school," asked a mom in the front row.

Very quietly from the back of the hall, "Howz 'bout a Sunday and we would tell the story of the Creator and the Creation?" asked Percy. "Why we could all git tugetther 'nd pray and praise, 'n sing somma them hymns what tells 'bout glory and God's beauytiful creeatiooon…..?" Beatrice sat there with Nevaeh on her lap. They were smiling all over. Her job had been to get all those who had participated in any way, especially the artists, to find a little spot to sign their name on the railcar. Some painted in corners on the outside; some typed on a little card and pasted it in the classroom. Soon their signatures became part of the beautiful design.

Silence filled the hall. Folks began to look at each other, remembering why the story was even painted on the railcar/center.

"Right how about October 4, the Feast of St. Francis? He loved Creation and, of course, the Creator! We will send invitations to all the churches and pastors and invite everyone from the county and town. We will even invite some folks from MSU and Ole MS to come. Mrs. Pluckworth has an invitation list so do put down anyone you want specially invited. Ideas came from all over the hall… articles in the newspapers… gather at 11am and praise our Creator together. Then we will declare *THE DOGWOOD STARS SCIENCE CENTER* officially open. Mayor will you get the red ribbon? Ms. President will you bring the scissors? Then we'll eat! Howz all this sound?"

A roar of applause filled the hall. Folks stood and cheered because *their* science center would be a place both of on-going learning, as well as praise for the Creator. The fact that the Creator created in six days did not mean He was all done! Meeby God was jist begin'in!

On the northern end of the railcar, looking out over the tracks, the tiny town of Castle, and toward the heart of the County, Alcor painted some very beautiful stars and this saying from the Scriptures:

> *"The wise shall shine brightly, like the splendor of the firmament, and those who lead the many to justice shall be like the stars forever."* (Dan 12:3)

My. My. My. Beautiful. *THE DOGWOOD STARS SCIENCE CENTER.* Think of all the beauty that will be discovered there! Who wouldda ever thought that a tiny community would pull together and renovate an old railcar? Things of great worth and longevity can happen when folks say *yes* to creativity and goodness.

THE END

4

Astra Fisic Meets Sacagawea

Curious how Sunday morning can bring friends together. For example, Melodious, Sarahfinna and Whiplash meet Astra Fisic at Thee Café and discuss the worries of the world, the nosey bits about the neighbors, (*ooops*), and what Astra Fisic might be up to with her 'grumpy' friends and a new project. The last one, the painting of the railcar, was a dooozy! Alcor was her own kinda star! Of course, they ate a lovely breakfast while they chatted. Beatrice, Percy and Nevaeh were getting on nicely. The quilting club continued and many of the women had gone on to do great things! Lots of volunteers at the science center. After breakfast, they headed out to the church of their choice. There were several different denominations among these friends!

++

Astra Fisic, a slightly retired astronomer, who almost always wears a red hat, was back at the park one Saturday morning. Percy and Nevaeh were walking around, playing with a frisbee and chasing a little pit bull puppy named Fax. He didn't look like much, really rather scrappy. He was rescued from a puppy mill, by his person Rockwell, who lives across the street from the park. Fax was whimpering and afraid and hidden under the fax-machine in the puppy mill's garage. Nevaeh was fascinated and the little puppy was gentle and playful with her. They seemed meant to be great friends.

Rockwell, would you believe this, was a teacher of science at the local community college! Yes, he taught geology, astronomy and physics. He and Astra Fisic became friends. He met her the first time at the Opening of the *The DOGWOOD STARS SCIENCE CENTER* in Castle and was so impressed he went back to teaching. Rockwell had been rather ill and was unable to work, but he could read and study, and read and study and that's what he did for a while. While he was healing he discovered coin collecting…well, he started by collecting the *FIFTY STATE, District of Columbia & Territorial* quarters. Recently he began to find the *NATIONAL PARK* quarters. Then he found Fax and his heart was even happier. Rockwell had someone to take care of and the puppy had a forever home. So Saturdays became special days Astra Fisic met her friends Rockwell and Fax at the park and they discussed astronomy, physics, geology and coin collecting. Well, not Fax he played with Percy and Nevaeh.

++

One Saturday Astra Fisic brought some of her coin collection to show Rockwell.

"Have you seen this one?" she balanced the coin on her hand. It was very shiny and though she found it in some change, Astra thought it was almost uncirculated.

"No, let's see," Rockwell turned to his collectors folder. "I don't have that one."

There was a most beautiful *Hot Springs P 2010*…the very first one in the National Park folder, stretching from 2010 to 2021! "Why Nevaeh will be four!" they laughed. "Don't know 'iffin I'll still be around to collect the last one, *Tuskegee Airmen D 2021*." Her eyes twinkled.

Rockwell asked, "You know I'm new to all this, what's that *D* and *P* mean?"

She had been collecting coins for about twenty years but she didn't know everything, but she did know that.

"Well, my friend, good question! The *D* (unless you have a very rare coin from Dahlone, GA, 1838-1861) comes from our Denver Mint. It started up in 1906 and continues to this day. The *P* started, git ready, in 1792, the very first US mint, in Philadelphia. These are markers to tell us where the coin was born. The latest mint is in West Point, NY and it began in 1984. I've never seen a coin with that mark though. You?"

"Nah, I have trouble keeping my *P*'s and *D*'s organized!"

++

Nevaeh and Percy swung by with Fax at their heels. "We're so hungry," they complained. "Got anything to eat?"

"Well, let's see." Astra was secretive as she carefully pulled out all the picnic stuff. "First I've something very special for Fax." She called him over and unveiled her official first batch of Fax-Biscuits. They were square, some were round, others triangles and even some very long ones. Astra Fisic made them from the same dough so as far as she knew, they all tasted the same. Fax was very interested and she let Percy feed some to him. Before she could get the blanket and tablecloth spread, Fax wanted more. Pumpkin, berries, and a little sweet potato with chicken bits bound together in a chicken broth and baked to cookie perfection made them disappear like winners!

"These look so good, I want to eat one!" Percy kidded with Astra.

"Well, go ahead, won't kill ya!"

So Percy ate a little triangle and Fax cocked his head as if to say... what??? *My* cookie-biscuits! "Very yummy, but what else is in your people-basket?"

Astra Fisic, Percy, Nevaeh and Rockwell discovered the chicken sandwiches with cucumbers and a little mayo; baked potato chips and some apple slices, along with a sweet potato salad (yes, that's right, sweet po). De-lish. None of it lasted long as they were all hungry.

"For dessert," she announced, "we have some blackberry cobbler made with biscuits and hand-picked by my friend Melodious. (We have available a squirt of whipped cream). We also have some chunks of white chocolate sent to me by my friend Hilda in Belgium. I can guarantee a tasty end to our picnic! Oh, to drink we have water, flavored water, apple juice, or coke."

"I brought something to eat as well," reported Rockwell and he handed each a little package. Nevaeh gurgled a bit, and played with her slurpee-go-gurt- squeeze. Quite a lot had ended up on her face but she smiled it away.

Astra and Percy were very curious. What might it be? They felt it and smelt it and then they started to open it when Rockwell challenged, "Wait a minute. Can you guess first? Let's see who get's the closest."

Astra and Percy looked at each other. Percy went first. "Well, it feels like a candy bar."

"Close but, no."

Astra was wiggling hers here and there and trying to get an idea from the lovely fragrance. "Well, I'm going to guess cake, some kinda cake?"

"Well, yer both kinda close. Open and see and then I hope you will enjoy eating it!" Rockwell smiled and handed Fax another Fax-Biscuit.

"Oh, my," Astra said as she tasted the wonderful creation Rockwell had baked. Percy hardly spoke but her face filled with 'yummy' and that was enough.

"This is my favorite (very special recipe for) double chocolate chip brownies with pecans and walnuts, topped with white chocolate chips." Rockwell beamed, feeling quite proud that his new friends like his creation so much.

++

Lunch had ended with such a wonderful surprise from Rockwell so he and Astra returned to their coin collection. Percy, Nevaeh and Fax went off running and jumping elsewhere.

"I heard they used coins when they buried people," Rockwell said. "I read something about that on the internet."

"Yes, me too. When the Greeks died, a coin was placed in the mouth of the deceased and that paid the ferryman, Charon, who rowed the newly dead across the River Styx. I think the first coins were Greek around 7thC BC." Astra was having such a very good time. She was happy to have friends like Rockwell and Fax. They helped her continue to learn to become a good friend.

"I heard that after Abe Lincoln was assassinated someone put coins over his eyes," he recounted.

"Really?" Astra had never heard that before.

"One of the things I find really interesting," Astra was on a roll, "is that each country eventually marked their coins with an emblem that meant something to them. Of course, the amount was important, but it might be their flag, or nature, or their leaders (most use 'dead' ones), or even places. Thomas Jefferson established the decimal monetary system to replace 'pounds' that were British. That meant that $1=100cents. There was a Congressional Resolution, April 6, 1792, to establish the US Mint. On the obverse side of the coin would be the emblem *LIBERTY* and the year of coinage. On the reverse for gold or silver would be a US eagle. On copper coins would be the denomination. David Rittenhouse was the first Director of the Mint and the first US coin was named the ½ Disme. It was silver and inscribed on the reverse. Gosh, I sound like I'm giving a lecture." They laughed.

"The *National Parks*, too, are great examples of places our country is proud of and these coins are such works of art! The other folder you and I did was the *States and Territories*. Do you know I have been collecting that folder since 1999 when it began? I have both *D* and *P* in my folder…and I cannot find *Guam P 2009*, the last one. Ugh. I have looked everywhere. I watch in change when I get quarters to do my laundry. I have even looked at the bank. But, no. I think that's a long time, why 18 years lookin' fer that one last coin to fill out my collection. Whadddya think?"

Rockwell looked at her with a very big smile. "Are we going to meet again next week?" he asked.

"Don't know why not unless I'm in glory!"

"OK." Rockwell had an idea. He said nothing more.

++

Percy, Fax and Nevaeh were headed in their direction in a big hurry.

Rockwell and Astra Fisic had packed up their coin folders and had already changed the subject to the total eclipse of the sun. Percy pulled up with Nevaeh asleep in the push-chair.

"Look at this," she said quickly producing a copperish-looking coin, maybe a bit bigger than a quarter but not as big as 50-cent piece. "What is it?"

"Oh my, where did you find this?" Astra was looking carefully.

"Over there we were just fooling around with the frisbee and when I went to get it to throw to Fax, this coin was peeking out from under a little lump of dirt."

"Well, my girl, first off, you've found a dollar! Used to be we'd only find pennies…now with inflation…*hahahahaha*." Rockwell laughed right out loud.

"Anyway, Rockwell, whaddya think?"

"Yea, it is a dollar and it has a woman on it."

"Well, I only know something about this because I collected a little folder in 2000 (a celebration of the Millennium) when it was first circulated. You know how we were talking about putting important people on our coins? Well, most have been men. This one is a very important young woman, a Shoshone Indian named Sacagawea."

"Well, is it rare, worth a lot?" Percy was hoping since she had discovered it.

"No, just a dollar, but the history of Sacagawea is worth noting. We also have another woman on a dollar coin, Susan B. Anthony."

Percy was pleased to have found a dollar and showed some interest in the woman's history. But really she was hoping to have found a rare coin worth lots of money. Not this time. Oh well.

++

They finished packing-up and Rockwell went home with Fax. Nevaeh was a bit cranky and needed to finish her nap on a bed. Astra Fisic put on a pot of tea and went to her room. Percy flopped onto the recliner and was almost asleep when Astra brought in her little three page cardboard folder about the $1.

"Thought you might like to read this yourself, I'm sorta outta lectures!" Percy nodded and thanked her. Astra brought in some mint tea and they relaxed. Actually, they both fell asleep and only awoke because they heard the plaintive pleas of Nevaeh. She was clearly done with her nap, never mind the rest of them! The phone rang and it was Beatrice on her way over to pick them up. Percy looked forward to showing the Sacagawea dollar coin to Beatrice so she carefully put it in her pocket.

Percy yawned and stretched and headed for Nevaeh's bed, changed her and hugged her a lot. They were sweet sisters. It was hard to believe where they'd come from. But, that's another story.

THE END

5

Astra Fisic @ 'the dogwood'

There was bustling and shuffling of chairs and tables as the folks moved here and there looking for a place to sit for the *DOGWOOD STARS SCIENCE CENTER Lecture#9*. It was a marvel, this science center classroom carved out of an old railcar renovated by Astra Fisic, Alcor, and their wonderful team from the town and county. They could not have been more proud and here it was almost two years later that she had opened.

Everyone knew Astra Fisic, the slightly retired astronomer with the red hat and now they knew Alcor (named after the constellation), Beatrice, Percy, Nevaeh, Rockwell and Fax. Astra Fisic's three grumpy friends, Melodious, Whiplash and Sarahfinna were happily in attendance. They liked to 'hear her talk,' they said in unison. "Always learn sumptun' from her!"

Star gazing, the basics of physics, little collections of bugs, rocks and butterflies, why, just about anything you might be interested in showed up in the science center lecture series. There were the fall ones and the spring ones. The summer was devoted to a sort of on-going *science* VBS. Astra Fisic was particularly tender when she thought about, prayed to, or shared with others the Creator, and she made sure that anyone who came to any lecture, though she did not give them all, was also very thoughtful of the Creator.

The local newspaper had written an article about #9 encouraging folks to attend. Apparently, something had been found that would *WOW!* them all. A special *DOGWOOD STARS SCIENCE AWARD* would be given to the young girl who found it. Astra Fisic also saw the lecture advertised on the local news. She hoped that it was going to be as exciting as everyone seemed to think. She was excited and had been there for the find…

++

Folks came from all over for these lectures and workshops. Before *'the dogwood'* (as it was frequently referred to) a Director was appointed because the artists and scientists had to keep doing their own work. The kids had to go back to school and the teachers had to prepare their lessons. Astra Fisic had invited seven folks to be a little Stars Board back when they began. They choose a Director after a long time of searching. The Director would receive a salary and so would the part-time secretary. The deputy director was a voluntary position.

Astra Fisic always introduces the part-time secretary first because she says she does all the work! Her name is Percy. Yes *our* Percy and what a very good job she is doing as she continues to go to college. The voluntary deputy Director is someone you also know, Rockwell, the scientist and college professor and person of Fax.

Then she introduced the Director, Dr. Hanna Edana, originally from Choctaw County, who rolls over in her electric bright agate orange all-mod-cons wheelie chair, and parks next to Astra Fisic. Both are beaming, as it is hard to believe this is really lecture #9! Hanna (meaning blest by God) Edana (meaning fiery) is looking out over the crowd as it begins to hush. Neighbors greet neighbors and some even share a cuppa. Folks new to 'the dogwood' continue to look at all the displays and the special cases and cabinets that tell the story of just how they got there.

"Well, Mizz Director, whaddya think? Looks like another sell-out crowd!"

"Yup," and they laugh because all the lectures are free. "I am so pleased to be here to hear your rather adventurous story. I know these folks are going to be very surprised!"

++

Dr. Hanna Edana was born in Choctaw County, well, I mean her family lived there. She was actually *born* in Jackson, MS, because prior to her birth some issues were discovered and the doctors knew she would need extra help. Hanna would never walk, not in this life anyway. She might trip and tumble as a toddler and even take a few steps with a stick or crutch as a youngster but she would live her life somewhere between her wheelie and her bed and she would not always be happy about it.

Her parents were very understanding and patient but it was not easy for them either. They wished she would be able to 'outgrow' her cerebral palsy (as a rather uninformed worker at the disability office seemed to think she would). Hanna had two brothers and a sister. She was the baby. Her sister was seven years older and they didn't always get along. Her brothers were ten and twelve years older and so she didn't know them very well though they played with her and cared for her when they were home. Then they left. Randy watched over Hanna as best she could when their mother was very ill. After she died, Hanna was about ten, Randy and their father decided to put Hanna in a group home for the handicapped. Hannah did not want to go but she knew that they were unable to provide the care she needed. They promised to visit frequently and they did.

++

Jackson Rocks was the name of the place, a really good group home if you could not be at your own. Yes, you read that right. Her father had known a guy when they were in college who became a priest. He phoned him and they talked off and on about the best possible place for Hanna who was very smart and really needed to go to college. What college? Well, get out your cow-bells and ring them loudly all the way to the doors of MSU! Hanna had passed all her high school work with no problem. She had some assistance from a teacher-tutor hired by the district. When it came time, she helped Hanna take all her exams and she graduated sixth in her class of forty-eight.

From the time she went to *Jackson Rocks*, Hanna wanted to study some kind of science (she also did art). She wasn't quite sure exactly what kind…maybe astronomy or geology or even physics. She was curious about her own limitations and wanted to study anatomy to see if she could find a cure. She was bit all over the place until she met Astra Fisic who at that time was teaching at MSU in the astronomy department. She came over to *Jackson Rocks* on occasion and got to know some of the residents. She and Hanna hit it off. Hanna was sixteen and finishing her junior year of HS.

In her senior year, her father passed and she and Randy were family. Randy had married and had a little boy who loved Hanna so much. They visited a lot and Randy was very insistent Hanna go to college. She got a dorm room and a roommate who doubled for her care-giver. They are still 'besties'. Hanna and Alma (means soul) both ended up getting their licenses to teach HS and elementary science. Alma went into junior high math and Hanna went on to teach community college classes for over five years after receiving her PhD. They stayed friends with Astra Fisic.

++

Hanna was thirty when she applied for the job as Director of *THE DOGWOOD STARS SCIENCE CENTER* and though she was very qualified was not so sure she'd get the job. The renovation of an old railcar into a science center was just so cool, she thought. Why it even has the best ramp-up-'n-in, she'd ever seen. There was a little office off and behind some display cases and her wheelie would fit just fine. Some adjustments could be made to the desk and other furniture to make it easier for her and her visitors to be more comfortable. Hanna really wanted the job. The seven members of the Stars Board agreed to take six qualifying candidates and over a period of days to discuss various things with them and hope that just the right person would become their Director. The days were full of discussions, presentations, and individual interviews. Hanna was the only one in a wheelie but one very knowledgeable young man, a veteran, was blind in one eye.

The Chairman of the Board, Rockwell, told the participants that they would make their decision and inform them in the next three working days…that meant five days because it was the weekend. Folks agreed, had a nice lunch together and dispersed. The rest is history, as they say. Dr. Hanna Edana was selected as the very first Director of *'the dogwood'* and she is still serving,

++

The room was almost full (chairs available for fifty) and Hanna was about to begin sharing some housekeeping instructions, where the bathrooms were, drink machine, hearing assistance table with headsets, and the bits of information about the center, when Astra Fisic and her three grumpy friends arrived. Sarahfinna, Whiplash and Melodious all found chairs and Astra wandered up to the front table and had a few words with Hanna. They looked at each other with bit of surprise and Hanna continued.

"Good evening all. I am so pleased to be welcoming you to '*the dogwood*' for Lecture #9 and the awarding of our very special science prize to Ms. Abigail Stocker, of the eighth grade class at our junior high school. Her science teacher Ms. Amy Wellborne, is also going to be with us for the presentation, as well as Abigail's mom, Mary."

"Before Dr. Astra Fisic gets underway with Lecture #9 I want to thank our Board for all the work they have done over the past two years, but especially this last year. They are indeed, stars! You might have noticed the '*ractor 'n 'ruck park*' surrounding our property? So named by little David Spencer, who is four, when his mom brought him over to visit. Why the antique 'ractors and 'rucks have all been donated by local farmers and pick-up folks. David is having a little speech therapy to try to get those '*trs*' going and that will be a very good thing. However, we have decided to name the park '*ractors 'n 'rucks*' in his honor!" David smiled and stood up with his mom.

"You have noticed the ecumenical nature of the tractors and pick-ups...John Deere's 1973, '4630' in its pristine green; the Kubota '13710' from 2002, bright orange; the Ford '4000' from 1998; Massey Ferguson's red 1988 Ferguson '590'; and the International Harvester's red 1952 Farmall Super 'A'. The pickups are almost as exciting. We have room for maybe three more so if anyone knows of one over twenty-five years old (that's around 1992) do donate. Check out the 1970 Chevrolet C20 in green and white; the 1971 D2000 brown Power Wagon; and the 1979 Lil Red Express. They have all been secured and made kid-safe and can be climbed on, driven (in place, of course) and dreamed in, with minimum supervision." There was a huge applause.

"I must get on," Hanna exclaimed as she looked at her *WONDER WOMAN* watch. "Why, we have so much to do. First, I am going to invite Dr. Astra Fisic, our slightly retired astronomer with her red hat, to come forward for Lecture #9 and tell us something about *MS Gravel Pits* and the surprising fossils found within them. Then we will be greeting a very special guest who will present our science award to Ms. Abigail. Thanks to all who brought food to share! I saw some very spectacular dishes over yonder and we want to eat it all! Bless your hearts!" Hanna putted over to the far side of the sorta-stage and Astra moved up to the podium. Her power point was ready and the lights went down.

"Good evening all. I am so glad to be with you again to share something I just love. Fossils. Maybe I'm even a fossil!" Folks laughed. "Anyway those fossil 'ractors and 'rucks show us the beauty of something kept in good condition as well as the evolution to even more beautiful and powerful tractors and trucks."

"Fossils are millions and even billions of years old as we know. Here are some pics of fossils often found in gravel in MS. The Silurian are some 439 million and the Mississippian are around 323million years old." She gently forwarded the pictures until she reached some of the various shapes.

"You can see from this picture how the streams rounded the pebbles and there are also spheroids, discs, blades and rollers. Some of these have traveled all the way down from the Nashville Dome in TN to the Appalachian Mountains of Alabama. All the ancient rivers were moving toward the Gulf and some of their deposits are still to be discovered in our hills in the gravel deposits of Northeast MS. They say that these ancient gravel deposits were recycled by erosion and that made up the new bars in modern rivers, like the Tombigbee."

Astra continued for about ten more minutes sharing about flint and especially petrified wood, and then began her favorite part. "Now as I conclude I must tell you all about agates. I just mentioned that many of the fossils we find were transported from other states as rocks imbedded in floating ice. Yes, floating ice. Even the tiny Mississippi proetid triobites you see in this picture. Now look at this."

OOOOs and *ahhhhas* filled the room as Astra showed the pictures of the beautiful agates. "Now, you might think that the Lake Superior agate, more often found in our gravel pits, are the only ones. But look here. This is a *Mississippi agate*. This agate was found by our own Ms. Abagail Stocker." Clapping and cheering followed.

"Abigail would you come up and help me tell these nice folks about Mississippi agates?"

Abigail came forward, a little shy leaning on her elbow-crutch, but clearly chuffed that she had found this 3" thunder-egg turtle-shell shaped MS agate. She had the real thing in her hand and would gladly show it around later.

"In 2013 I read an article by Karli Duron on *HubPages* and from that time on was determined to find a MS agate. Our eighth grade science trip down to the Natchez Formation to find a Lake Superior agate was unsuccessful. So we wandered back up this way and found a large gravel pit and decided to just give it a chance. Maybe we would find what we were looking for. Abigail had strapped on her brace and clutched her crutch, and set off like rocket onto the shifting rocks and pebbles of the gravel pit. The other children, some of you are here tonight, began sifting and picking up and looking for the right colors and sizes and shapes we had studied. It was a very big pit and the day was drawing to a close. We needed to get back home. You tell what happened next."

"Well, I was so determined to find a MS agate," began Abigail, "well, so I just kept looking. I knew Dr. Astra wanted us to go but I, well, just couldn't. I had a bowl with me and so I just scooped up as much as I could, well, fit into it and slowly looked at each and every rock, large and small. As I got to the bottom of the bowl well, I found a sort of thunder-egg but it had a shape that reminded me of my turtle. It was cracked open on one side so the colors were visible. I took a big breath. Did I really find something like an agate? Then I called over to Dr. Astra and, well, she came running. I think she thought I had fallen and was hurt. Anyway, when she got there, well, I handed her the egg. She called everybody over and we went over the list of things that would, well, make finding a MS agate easier to detect in the field. And sure enough, bless our hearts, we had found a genuine MS agate!" Abigail could not stop smiling and holding the agate up for all to see. Astra moved over to hug her.

"I want to just add a bit to that as we close and then introduce the special guest who is going to give our Abigail her award."

"Agate means 'happy' and we could not have been happier for Abigail and our class to discover this one among millions of pebbles and rocks just on that one gravel dump along the MS River basin. Agates are precious stones. As you can see the beauty of an agate is born by colors, usually rust-red from the oxidizing iron or even yellow, brown, black, grey, pink, and even sometimes green. White bands of quartz separate the colors and the colors are the stain from the iron. The translucence of the quartz allows the light to shine through and even glow. Ours glows! Agates are embedded in volcanic matter and maybe you don't know this, but there is an extinct volcano 2,900' below the Jackson, MS, coliseum. Yes, indeedie. It has been extinct for over 65 million years and last erupted 75million years ago. Not to worry. Unlikely to blow again. But what it does mean, is that deep down there must be many more MS agates yet undiscovered! Who wants to go looking?"

Hands went up and folks could hardly believe that the hour lecture, turning closer to an hour and a half, was over. Now, who was this special presenter?

Hanna drove over and took center stage, and invited Abigail, her mom and teacher to come and stand next to her.

"Ladies and Gentlemen, it is my joy to introduce to you the Governor of the Great State of Mississippi, the Honorable Jasmine S. Evans, born in Choctaw County." The room hushed as the Governor came out from Hanna's office. Governor Jasmine was of medium height and wore a gracefully tailored grey pantsuit showing off her nut-brown skin. Around her neck was a very colorful lightweight scarf and her heels drew out the red in it. Her glasses were frameless and she wore a small silver cross. She was full of smiles and waves and the people were so proud to be with her. Jasmine had been Governor for two years and folks said, so far, so good. In her hands, she carried two items. One was *THE DOGWOOD STARS SCIENCE CENTER AWARD* and the other...well...couldn't quite tell.

"Thank You Dr. Hanna and Dr. Astra and all your wonderful folks. What a special night we are celebrating, in my home County. I just wish I could have seen all those pictures Astra showed you! Abigail I am so proud of you. It was not so easy for you to climb up that hill and to keep looking for this MS Agate. Even though petrified wood is our state stone, I suspect this agate will be forever important here at *'the dogwood'.*" Folks clapped.

"On behalf of your center and school I would like to present you with this Stars Certificate and a *certificate of authenticity* received from MSU about the agate." Folks clapped again and some were even standing, stretching their necks trying to see better.

"Your perseverance and study has brought us this a 1B year old gift from the Creator. Mercy. Can you believe it? Thank you too for your family who has encouraged you in this study." She looked over at Abigail's mom, Mary. Abigail took the two certificates from the Governor, shook her hand, and handed them to her mother. They sat down.

"Finally I have something very special for you Dr. Hanna and your team here at *'the dogwood'*. I had hoped to get home for your Opening but it was just around the election and pressing matters held me up. Please find a suitable place within this wonderful railcar center for this little plaque from me and the State of Mississippi honoring y'all for all your hard work and scientific fun. Please continue and next time I'm back home in Choctaw I'll come by for a visit! We need to relive our high school days!" Hanna stayed put as Governor Jasmine brought her the plaque. They hugged. What a photo-op for the local newspapers, and what a thrill for Abigail, and all those on the MS agate find.

Lecture #9 was over. The Governor stayed on awhile before heading back to Jackson and all the food mysteriously disappeared. Really? Naw. Everybody ate until there was nothing left but hugs and good-byes until Lecture #10 coming up in about five months. Even Astra's three grumpy friends were warming up to the idea that grumpy was not always the best way to go! Everyone paused and ended with a big thank you to the Creator remembering far back in Exodus times:

> "*The breastplate of decision you shall have made...on it you shall mount four rows of precious stones: in the first row, a carnelian, a topaz, and an emerald; in the second row, a garnet, a sapphire, and a beryl; in the third row a jacinth,* <u>an agate</u>, *and an amethyst; in the fourth row, a chrysolite, an onyx and a jasper...each stone engraved like a seal with the name of one of the twelve tribes.*" (cf Ex28:15ff)

Y'all come back!

THE END

6

Astra Fisic and the Other Brothers

Almost any Sunday morning just around 8:30AM or so you'll find Sarahfinna, Whiplash, Melodious and Astra Fisic, slightly retired astronomer and wearer of a red hat, eating breakfast at Thee Café before going to church. Sometimes Alcor joined them, or ChaChalita or Joyus from the quilt club. Even if no one else was in Thee Café, these four were, discussing the week's news, whatever project they might be working on, and eating a tall-stack with scrambled eggs and crispy bacon. It was the Sunday before Fat Tuesday, Ash Wednesday and the beginning of Lent. (Well, at least for Astra Fisic and Melodious where such things celebrated). They ate up!

They did not all go to the same place of worship and since this county had so many churches it was hard to choose 'iffin you'd not been brought up in one particular one like Astra Fisic. Now she is a Catholic. Then there's Whiplash who prefers the Presbyterians, Melodious a Methodist, and Sarahfinna tends more toward the Pentecostals. You might think those three, being sisters, might be in the same worship family. But, no, they grew up sorta together and sorta not. Anyway, they said that the preacher made a *big* difference.

Bro. Tim from the Presbyterians was a quiet, gentle sorta guy with a lovely wife and four very little children. He was a good preacher, especially because he was short and to the point, Whiplash pointed out. She liked things that moved along.

The Methodist pastor Rev. Peterpaul was a different sorta guy. He loved all styles of church music and Melodious (despite her tone-deafness) loved her choir! He included as many songs as possible in their worship time and even though he was a good preacher, he was, in fact, a better singer. Melodious said it was like hev'en when he sang. His wife was very energetic and made sure there were many projects members could get into to help others. They have three kids.

Bro. Rudy was hot. He was very handsome and the girls sat in the front row just to watch him gyrate and wipe the sweat from his forehead. They loved their pastor and he loved them. When Bro. Rudy was preachin' and on a roll, why the Holy Ghost was most assuredly present; it seemed even more unquestionable when he lifted his Bible and shook it. His wife was a bit timid and their two tween children, very well behaved. He had only been a preacher for about three years. He did not go to a seminary but felt God call him and up he got, off he went, and here he is.

Fr. Frank, the Catholic priest, was a charming fellow from Kenya. Right. Not a local fellow. He had been at the Catholic Church for only two years but Astra thought he was brilliant. He had a wonderful sing-song lilt to his voice and struggled with his accent a little. Up to the folks to learn to listen to him, Astra mentioned, not all on him to git it right. He had a very funny sense of humor, and when Frank preached, he frequently told a story or two that reminded folks about the Gospel or one of the other readings. Astra loved his stories. Frank was not the pastor. He was the 'sacramental minister'.

The pastor was Ms. Donna, a Choctaw woman. Really? Yup. Fr. Frank was *a* pastor but down in another county and he came to celebrate the sacraments at Astra's church each week. During the week and most of the time, Ms. Donna pastored. Astra loved her a lot and was happy to serve with her visiting the sick and the women up at the jail. Women aren't ordained priests so if there is a priest close enough, he comes for certain celebrations. Partly this is because we're so out in the country but it happens in cities as well. Ms. Donna could do the other celebrations and bring the community together for all their ministries. And could she preach? Yes, she could and she did very well, especially the Wednesday night services. She'd had her training and lots of experience over the years. She had compassion and could manage folks with very different ideas. She didn't realize how much of a gift she was to her little community.

++

Sunrise on the Arizona desert is usually colorful and magnificent especially in spring. This morning it was uncharacteristically wet, raining bigly. The four young men gathered in their tiny chapel for prayer. The rain pelted down on the metal roof and they could hardly hear one another, as prayers were prayed and the songs sung. When they finished they adjourned to the small kitchen for breakfast and a little meeting.

"We're just about ready to set out," Br. Andrew said, "Mississippi seems so far away but we can make it. Tomorrow is Ash Wednesday and our goal is to arrive on Good Friday in Tatersville near McCool, MS. Forty days, mas or menos." You might wonder why they chose Mississippi. Well among many reasons, Rev. Peterpaul had been an *Other Brother* some years ago before he married and finished seminary. He knew the *Other Brothers'* pastor and had contacted him last year. Where were the *Other Brothers* going on their pilgrimage? Nowhere yet chosen? Well, what about Mississippi? Perfect, for their penitential focus on racism and inclusion.

"Not sure how many miles that actually is, but walking and carrying a full size Cross...well," Br. Richard smiled and was ready to go.

Brothers Henry and Butch had begun doing dishes and asked about the packing yet to be finished before a 6am departure.

"Are we leaving even if this rain continues?" Br. Butch asked, almost hoping Andrew would say no.

"Of course." They hand bumped one another and began their chores.

Br. Butch set out for the barn where Williemeanna lived. She was their donkey and would be a working traveler. Br. Butch was primarily responsible for her so he had begun to lay out all her blankets, bags, and leathers. She knew something was up and trusted Butch.

++

Easter would be, let's see, April 12 this year so Good Friday was the 10th. If you were part of the Tatersville Community Church you would be looking for the *Other Brothers* arrival, including their donkey Williemeanna. Rev. Peterpaul, Bro. Tim, Bro. Rudy, and Ms. Donna (Fr. Frank would come if he could) were having a meeting to discuss how they might welcome the *Other Brothers* who were walking in prayer and penance from Arizona.

They would be sharing with folks along the way, the evils of racism and the declared supremacy of any group set on excluding or terrorizing others. These attitudes were not Christian. Br. Andrew is African-American, Br. Butch, Anglo, Brs. Henry and Richard, Latinos (though their roots are in two different countries.). They tried to live out each day this cultural mix in their own lives so that they could remind people why Jesus was crucified. He did not fit. He spoke truth to power. He welcomed everyone. He even invited folks to do good to their enemies. Imagine!

++

You might be wondering who these *Other Brothers* are? These four belong to a world-wide community of brothers of different Christian denominations. Each one has his own religious family but together they are the *Other Brothers*, young men in their mid-late 20's who want to give two years to inter-faith community, prayer and sacrifice. In their second year, these four were *seconds*, a pilgrimage of some sort was planned. The one chosen this year was to walk across the SW deserts into the Deep South where they would arrive in Tatersville, Mississippi, witnessing to the gift of the Crucified Christ. This included carrying a life-sized Cross, in rotation, as they walked. Williemeanna carried their few possessions and was a most charming visitor especially for the children. The brothers tried to convince the kids that this was the very donkey Mary and Joseph used to escape to Egypt with baby Jesus! Not likely. All laughed.

Despite their difference in some doctrine and liturgical practice, these guys shared in the one Jesus Who was the center of their community life. When they completed this pilgrimage, their two years would be complete and they would return to their own home communities. The guys were looking forward to meeting up with their brothers in Tatersville.

++

Astra Fisic was very excited about the coming of the *Other Brothers*. It was a perfect opportunity, like the Opening of *'the dogwood'*, three years ago, to thank the Creator. Why all the churches could gather again for the day and a night of celebration and prayer as these young men reminded them of their Lenten practice and the amazing gift the Creator gave in His Son's crucifixion, death, and then ultimate resurrection. Oh my, just the thing for our county to gather again for praising and worship. These *Other Brothers* were famous for their music and so before they arrived Rev. Peterpaul shared around the churches some of their music, so everyone would be prepared to celebrate. He knew the music well. Closer to the time of arrival Peterpaul would hold a choir practice or three and then at least a number of folks would be prepared. The music was ever so easy and created a beautiful atmosphere for praising and prayer.

++

"Come on, Willie-girl," Butch begged her. She was not interested in getting stuck in the mud again. She did not move. They had walked their first 100 miles and it seemed a thousand. For several months, they had been walking and running to get into shape. The addition of the Cross increased the sacrifice and made the walk more difficult. Each man shouldered it for three hours at a time. He was clear where it had ground down into his body and at night when they stopped a good massage with oil was welcomed. Williemeanna was not moving. So everyone sat down, watching for puddles. The rain-storm seemed to have followed them but was beginning to lessen. The heat bubble, however, was not. Already 91degrees, by 10:30am.

Their habits were simple dusty-brown ankle-length hooded tunics, leather belt and small wooden Cross. They could choose between sandals and shoes and on this trip, ankle boots. Williemeanna was happy to carry their boots and change of clothes. A woven poncho, hat, sunglasses, and a 'do-rag', shorts, socks and a T-shirt completed the package. All layers seemed to stay wet, either from the rain or from sweat. This was not an easy walk.

++

The horns blared as the brothers had to walk along a pathway very close to the freeway. Williemeanna was not spooked but she clearly disliked all the noise. It hadn't been in their plan, so it took them longer to arrive at the next place. They were so glad to meet the folks on the far eastern border of Texas, near Tyler. Butch had begged some food for lunch yet they were very hungry.

The BBQ pit was fired up, and it was a cooler early evening than they had experienced since their pilgrimage began. Food was everywhere and so were the people of the *Mighty God Methodist AME Church* and their neighbors who had come to welcome these young men with lots of food and fun on the ground.

Bro. Ing had applauded them and introduced them to the four families who would host them. The little church had no hall or common place, except the church itself. The town, Yearly, was very tiny.

Butch and Williemeanna stayed just on the edge of town at a small farm where cotton was grown and he would learn later that the kind of cotton was different from the cotton he'd meet one day in Mississippi.

Butch, Richard, Henry and Andrew were received with open arms, baths, beds, comfy chairs, food, well, just about anything the family had to share. Buckets or bowls full of hot water, then cold water, then lukewarm water, with just a touch of aroma oil, just to soak aching feet. Williemeanna' treats were carrots and apples as well as a big bunch of hay. She was very pleased. The *Other Brothers* were so grateful. This was a two- day stop so after eating as much as they might they set off to their host's homes for a long night of relaxed sleep.

++

The pastor of Tatersville Community Church, Bro. John, was also hard at work. His partner Astra Fisic had driven down to his office. They were a much bigger church and had a very large life-center, as they called it. The floor was a soft indoor-outdoor carpet, and there were plenty of restrooms and the kitchen was full of all the mod-cons. This would be the *Other Brothers* last stop so they wanted it to be very special.

Decorations had begun (crosses made by the children). Astra filled Bro. John in on the other meetings.

++

The *Other Brothers* struggled as they moved around the city. Protestors were annoying in the least, with signs and loud language making fun of them and trying to annoy Williemeanna. When this happened, and it only happened a few times, they just broke into song and carried on. They had been walking over thirty days now and between blisters on their feet and sores on their upper bodies from the Cross, they were filled with a sort of peaceful joy. Each place they had stopped for the night the people had been wonderful. They prayed and praised together, as well as shared table fellowship and much music. It was hard to believe there were only ten days left to Good Friday. Would they make it to Tatersville on time?

++

Astra Fisic and her committee were also counting the days. She and some friends met at Thee Café for the *red-white-and-blue plate* lunch and talked about what was needed. Sarahfinna's welcome procession was almost organized. Melodious had the choir learning music and was ready for their coming.

++

The *Other Brothers* moved as quickly as they might but they were tired, sore and amazed. They sat down to eat a lunch Henry had begged, a few oranges, apples and bananas, as well as some peanut butter and a loaf of homemade bread. Andrew took out the map and spread it across the picnic table at the park. Williemeanna was happily grazing and the little park's grass would be well cut and tidied by the time she had finished.

"OK, we are here, almost at the Louisiana border headed for the City of New Orleans. This is a two day stop. From there we will cross the Mississippi River and head up state for Tatersville."

The brothers looked at one another and at the Cross. It was difficult to believe they had come this far. It made the rest of the trip seem very long. Perhaps this was one big waste of time, but no. They knew in their hearts that they had grown as men, as brothers, and they had grown as Christians. They had given over their lives to something ultimately important. Lots of things are important, few reach the 'ultimate' level. As they finished lunch, they packed up and were ready for another six hours before they'd look for a stopping place. Perhaps a church or hall, a school gym or an open field, it didn't really matter. God had provided a place every night during the pilgrimage and the people they met were really like angels sent to comfort them. What mattered was perseverance…they had to keep going, they had to carry their Cross. Butch was bearing it the next three hours.

++

The *Other Brothers* had phoned in on a borrowed phone when they reached New Orleans. Astra Fisic was getting so excited that soon and very soon they would be in Tatersville. She had prayed for them each day of Lent and knew that all the other folks in the county did as well. Someone had taken a photo of them walking, Cross and Williemeanna included, and emailed it to Astra. She took their notes and wrote an article for the paper and the editor gladly placed it on the front- page encouraging folks to set Holy Thursday night or Good Friday aside.

++

New Orleans included a long and cool visit to the Cathedral. Outside it was very stuffy with the humidity of a spring rain adding to their sluggishness. They separated and found their own special spot in the Cathedral and nestled down into the pew for a two- hour time of prayer. The coolness covered them and one by one they fell asleep for at least half an hour. Refreshed they returned to their prayer and reading of

Scripture. Later that evening Andrew would give a little talk, there would be music and Henry would lead some communal prayers. The Cathedral community was so welcoming and the *Other Brothers* found the pastor a real help.

Richard had badly turned his ankle during the last time he carried the Cross and they thought he needed a doctor. Msgr. Bill loaded them up into the church van and whisked them off to the free-clinic the cathedral sponsored. Dr. Aileen took some x-rays and reported only a slight fracture but a serious sprain. She bound the ankle in a support, offered him some pain-pills (he declined) and a shot (he accepted). Msgr. Bill had a cane from the thrift shop and that gave him a bit more support. The other brothers laughed when Msgr. Bill wanted to put him in a wheel chair. "I'll just hobble," he said feeling just a little sleepy from the injection. Dr. Aileen sent him to bed, reminding him to elevate the ankle as much as possible. She wasn't sure about walking the rest of the way to Tatersville. For sure he would not carry that Cross anymore. The other brothers would have to rotate sooner.

++

Richard's ankle proved a bit of a problem. He really did need assistance and so Williemeanna volunteered and became his best friend. She let him ride on her back. He felt a little anxious especially when a group of people gathered. He felt so tall. Never mind, God had provided Williemeanna and he was not going to complain. Most of the rest of the trip was in the country, off road, and Richard and Williemeanna would get along fine. The other brothers would carry his rotation of the Cross.

++

Sarahfinna met with the Tatersville Police Chief and the County Sheriff to make sure that the procession coming into town would be safe. Already it was Tuesday and the *Other Brothers* would be arriving either late Holy Thursday night or early Good Friday morning. They weren't quite sure yet. They had heard about Richard's accident. Some EMTs would assist him. They had decided to begin the welcome about 2 miles out of Tatersville along Hwy 411so everyone might be part of the procession into town. The people would gather there for prayer and just wait for the *Other Brothers*.

++

Andrew was carrying the Cross. He was not having an easy time of it. He had thought that nearing the end it would be easier as they had walked and carried, even drug, that Cross for so many miles. But not so for him. What to do, he wondered in his soul. Well from the top of his lungs, he belted out one of their favorite songs...*Sing of the Cross, That Strangest of Gifts*. Henry, Butch and Richard (and Williemeanna), were roused out of their mesmerizing walk, and joined in at full voice. There were no people to hear, only their sweet Jesus for whom this pilgrimage of gratitude had been taken. Not long now. Who would have thought?

++

Sarahfinna's welcome committee had their posters, music discs, bottles of water, and ambulance ready to go. The children had gathered, some with crosses of their own. The phone call had come and it looked like the *Other Brothers* would arrive Holy Thursday after six if all went well. So the committee decided to provide food as well as the table fellowship celebration. A farmer nearby would bring Williemeanna the best hay, apples, carrots, lots of cool water and anything else he might find.

++

Richard dismounted and Williemeanna was grateful. She wandered over to graze a bit and found some large tufts of grass just waiting for her to eat. The brothers sat down on some rocks.

"Well, this is the last few miles and we'll be in Tatersville, MS. I am finding it amazing. How about you?" Andrew asked.

Henry was so silent by nature but he was ready to talk and talk. "I'm really excited even though my body has taken some bad hits. I'm hungry and tired. Very tired. Equally, I am so amazed that we have had no fights, only a few disagreements on our travel path, and that our sweet Jesus has remained at the forefront of our journey. Bless Him."

Richard could only be grateful. Over and over he thanked his brothers for their care and love especially after the accident. They assured him it was because they loved him and that the extra carrying of the Cross was what the missionary disciple was to do for his neighbor. Go the extra mile? Well, what about nearly 200 miles? Tucson, maybe 2,000 miles away, was like a far way place in a dream. Even Jackson, MS, where they did their final prayer service and music presentation, seemed hundreds of miles away.

"I'd like to speak for myself and for Williemeanna. We have been so aware of the needs we have witnessed. Folks who were hungry, we ate in their soup kitchens. Folks who were afraid, we sat with them and prayed, and folks who were learning to love and praised with them. We read the Scriptures and sang our songs. We met the people of this country and though some were bound and determined to run us off the road, others reached out and helped us. We had to tell the evil one to go to 'hell' more than once. It is the only place he belongs! Oh, Willie-girl thanks us, and all our friends, for the great meals and just being with us. She is very fond of our love of Jesus and reminds us of her ancient cousin who *really did* carry Mary and the Child!"

Andrew led them in prayer and song. It was Wednesday night. They stayed in the field, ate lightly, and slept with expectation and joy.

++

Astra Fisic, Bro. John and all the others gathered at the life-center around 3pm, Holy Thursday afternoon. Sarahfinna gave some final instructions. Rev. Peterpaul went through some of the songs and they prayed. Around 4:30pm, they formed two long lines, the children in front, carrying their candles and began walking towards the *Other Brothers* who were nearing Tatersville. The brothers figured it was another seven miles to the meeting point. Henry had the Cross. They had tied some scarves on it graciously received at the Jackson rally. Stamped on them were sayings about ending racism, having hope, or just the word love. They blew in the gentle spring breeze. It was not humid and the brothers felt they could wander at speed without dying of the heat or swimming in the rain.

++

Close to 6pm, the *Other Brothers* could be seen coming up the road, Williemeanna in front with Richard on her back, then Henry with the Cross, and the people of Tatersville and the county began to rush towards them.

Astra Fisic was filled with the Spirit as the singers began to sing and the musicians began to play. They were meeting their sweet Jesus in the form of these brothers who had taken almost forty days to cross the deserts of the southwest and enter into the deep South, praying and doing penance for the sins of racism and exclusion, superiority and greed. The graces of their sacrifices would go to all of God's people as gifts from Jesus who said NO to these very things.

++

They met. Four other men stepped up and took the Cross. They represented the *Other Brothers* religious families. They were there to take them home. The EMTs helped Richard dismount and offered him some support.

Now they would share with the Tatersville community table fellowship for Holy Thursday. As the community ringed them round

Bro. John, Rev. Peterpaul, Ms. Donna, Fr. Frank, Bro. Tim and Bro. Rudy went to each of the four and washed their feet. Tomorrow they would all face the totality of the gift of the Cross. Tonight they would learn to take care of each other, to welcome the stranger and to feed the hungry. Tonight they would wait for the gift of the Cross to bloom in them.

Next year is the tenth year for the *Other Brothers* and the Superiors have decided the new group would invite a Muslim, a Jew and a Jehovah Witness to join the Catholic, Presbyterian, Methodist and Pentecostal. Their house and little farm near Tucson is big enough. Will their hearts be?

THE END

7

Astra Fisic and Hotdogs Rule: Little League Baseball

Nearing the end of the summer was pleasant for some and a disaster for others. School was coming whether you liked it or not. Sparepart did not like school. He was never quite sure how he made it all the way to the seventh grade without failing. All he could figure was that he loved baseball much more and dreamed of one day playing in Williamsport at the *Little League World Series* and pitching the final and winning game for the SE Team. His team, the *Hotdogs Rule,* never even made it to the local play-offs year after year and now that he was thirteen his dream seemed to be closing out.

Sparepart was Whiplash's nephew. And Whiplash was one of Astra Fisic's grumpy friends. Whiplash had had quite a good pitching arm herself growing up but girls had to play softball (that's another story). She played well but always wanted to throw that strong and curvy overhand fast-ball fading slider with a little float from the knuckles pitch of hers instead of the powerful full circle with that big fat ball. Their brother Thomas Junior was a decent athlete but had no interest in baseball. He played a little in school but became a bigtime fan when his son, Sparepart, was in T-ball. Thomas had never to this day missed a game and that's a lotta baseball. He had given him that nickname, as *Thomas Junior Junior* was a mouthful. Soon Whiplash and their other two sisters Melodious and Sarahfinna, also became supporters of Sparepart and his various teams. Coming late to Sparepart's career in Little League, was Astra Fisic their great friend, the slightly retired astronomer who wore a red hat. In fact, it was his last season.

++

It had been over four years since the Opening of '*the dogwood*' and there had been so many lectures, and summer programs and well just all sorts of wonderful events bringing the town and county together. The latest had been her summer film-series. She tried not to have the films compete with baseball but unfortunately, they sometimes did. The films were both interesting and educational.

As soon as she tried to schedule them for Wednesday nights, the churches moaned. OK, how about Tuesday nights? The Cub Scouts moaned. Then there was Thursdays and the 4-H moaned. Fridays, Saturdays (LL ball games) and Sundays were definitely o.u.t.

"OK, OK," she said, "last opportunity…the summer film series will be on Monday nights from 4:30pm-6:30pm. Bring a brown bag to share."

++

Sparepart liked movies so he was looking forward to going over to '*the dogwood*' for the series. Everybody in town rode a bike (at least all the kids) and there were plenty of bike racks in the lot. He heard there was to be a very big baseball movie and clips all about the *LL World Series*, the very first in 1947. In any case that one was single elimination, not like now, and it musta been something. For sure he'd go to that one. Astra Fisic, however, was not showing that one until very near the end of the film-series…and the end of the regular summer season for the oldest boys. She wanted it to be a sorta special. She would also be showing another movie from 1947 that she wanted the folks to take in. That was to be a real surprise, a double-header.

++

How many outs and how many strikes does it take to win a championship, a World Series? Astra wondered. She was a slightly retired astronomer but her math wasn't that strong anymore. Never mind, she thought. It takes a lot of cool heads and swift pitching. She had played a little but nothing like Whiplash.

++

Tony was the Castle High School baseball coach and this time of the year was always looking at the new boys soon to come to the junior/high school. Sparepart was certainly on his list. Tony had been lucky enough to play in the *LL World Series* in 1989 when his Team East won 5-2. It had been the LL's fiftieth anniversary and a special series. They beat Team Far East, Chinese Taipei, in a great upset.

He was from Trumbull, CT, and had moved south to Mississippi after college. He could only remember that day, when he was so small, playing in the last game, they were set for elimination. But no, he got a hit and the Blue Island East kids became the East going to Williamsport. He knew how much his coach had influenced him and given him confidence to even get out there and try. Now he tried to do that for other kids. Sometimes he was involved over the summer but this past summer he had married Terry Lee and they were busy doing other things. But now, school was about to start, so he was looking for new guys for his Castle High School team.

++

Astra Fisic was not happy. The films had not arrived and the day was soon approaching when she had promised to show the double-header. Over the summer, the movies had folks climbing Mt. Everest, playing in the 1960 Super Bowl, ducking under an hour of the Navy's *BLUE ANGELS* flying in formation, two hours of plain old cartoons…Daffy, Mickey, and all the rest. She also showed basketball and track, and a favorite movie of hers, *My Dog, Skip*, a Mississippi classic. Only one more week. She needed those movies! The big double-header was advertised and folks were planning on attending. For this one she was asking a donation and the money would go to the LL baseball program. Everyone can give a little and some can give more, she thought. What to do? Will the films show up?

++

Sparepart was up to bat. It was the top of the third and already they were down 4-0. He wasn't a great hitter and Coach Dan knew that he just needed to gain a little more confidence before he would bloom into a better player. Dan was very strict on his boys because he knew from experience what stress could do. Try-outs took several days even weeks sometimes if there were a plethora of boys for the teams. Sparepart got lucky and walked. The *Hotdogs* had their first base runner.

++

Sparepart was rising thirteen. It was his last chance at LL in the summer and the beginning of his 'big league career' at junior high school. The *Hotdogs Rule* were mostly all twelve and quite a few were trying out for Coach Tony at school. No one could remember in all their history of them winning much of anything. The team was founded in 1980, by *Joe the Hotdog Man*, and that year they won three games out of 15 (including a consolation game). In 1982, they won two and in 1997 they actually won five games. That year they had a very good pitcher and she helped a lot. Her name was Trakayla and she had a real arm on her! At first the boys balked at having a girl…soon, they begged her to pitch to them that they might improve their batting skills. Trakayla was tall and lean and powerful for an eleven year old. She had tried to play with another team or two but they rejected her, sarcastically sending her off to softball *where the girls belong.* She was not put off nor were her parents who encouraged her to find a team and go play.

She found *Hotdogs Rule,* tried out and was assigned to right field. Trakayla did mention to the coaches that she was a pitcher, but the boy-pitcher was so jealous he was like green pickle relish on a hotdog. Coach Dan was trying to man him up a bit before he took a chance on Trakayla. He tried matching Trakayla and Hermon for workouts who would refuse thinking, the other boys would make fun of him as he was already thirteen and it was his last season. Coach Dan would send Hermon out to pitch and the other team ate him up with homers, doubles and even walks. Finally, about halfway through the summer, Coach decided to start Trakayla. Her parents were in their usual place watching and her little sister kept yelling out her name. Her batting had improved a lot while playing right field and her arm strengthened because if the ball was coming her way and not a home run, she caught it and was able to deliver all the way to home plate. The catcher loved her junk.

Trakayla was a little nervous but she knew she had the stuff. Her fastball was very fast and very accurate. Her curveball needed some work but if she was lucky it would fool the batter a bit. Her favorite was a knuckle ball. Coach had never seen an eleven- year old throw a real knuckle ball. Her father had taught it to her and she watched that ball dance its way to home plate. Those little guys turned their heads and watched, not sure when or how to try to strike as it floated and bounced their way. She was ready.

Coach announced positions, had the little team chant, and gave the game ball to Trakayla.

"Girl, you go out there and throw yer best stuff. I wanna see some strike-outs and at the same time trust your defense. The boys are here to catch and throw out anyone that messes with you... got it?"

"Yea, Coach," she said with a quiet confidence and walked out to the dusty mound where the *Hotdogs Rule* were playing the *Bluebirds*, the team that was leading the league. Of all teams to bring it, her first start. Trakayla knew her routines and the catcher Chris had practiced with her for many hours since June. Now it was the end of July and if they were going anywhere this year they needed to git goin'!

Trakayla reared back and threw a fast ball. Strike! Chris nodded and they looked over at Coach Dan with the big smile on his face.

Go ahead, go ahead, just throw and enjoy, he signed over to them. From then on all the way to the end of the fifth Trakayla pitched her little heart out. Seven strike-outs for her first time out. Not bad! The *Hotdogs* won that day 1-0. An upset and the *Bluebirds* were very cross indeed! They were one of the teams that had rejected Trakayla!

++

Sparepart was bound and determined to be a champion. There was no reason, he thought to himself, that the *Hotdogs* weren't as good a team as anyone else, we just need a few breaks. The *MS Mockingbirds* were a formidable team, in fact third in the league and intended to stomp all over the *Hotdogs*. (They had considered changing their name when Joe, the Hotdog man passed, but felt the history was more important than the jabs they took). Sparepart, who had walked in the first, reared back and swung with all his might. Strike! One and one. The next two pitches were balls and Coach Dan gave him the swing away sign. He drew in his breath, he looked out at center field, well over 225' away, and imagined, envisioned, thought about hitting the ball all the way out there and how good it would feel to round those bases. And that is exactly what he did. The ball was coming fast and he knew all he had to do was put the bat out there, give it some direction and 'good-bye baby', it would go sailing into space. Pow, off it went with everyone turning around to watch her fly; pow, right over, well over, the homerun fence and Sparepart had his very best hit ever. There were two on so now they had three runs. 4-3 and no outs.

The next two batters were thrown out and then Moira came to the plate. Her cousin, Trakayla, had played for this team some years ago and now she would shine. The pitcher tried to stare her down. He didn't like girls playing with boys. Moira played shortstop and third base. She could pitch if absolutely necessary, but preferred shortstop, probably the position needing the most athletic ability and the most 'baseball-think'. She was short and twelve years old. She could run once she got going and had the stealing bases record for the *Hotdogs*. The pitcher reared back, it was 2-2, Moira watched carefully, stepped into it, swung her bat in the direction of the on-coming ball and sockooooo...it's outta here. Bye-bye baby! We have a ball game. 4-4. It was Moira's first homerun that season and as she rounded the bases she noticed someone in the stands near her dug-out who was not there at the beginning of the game. It was Trakayla!

++

Astra Fisic had learned a lot more about baseball this year as Sparepart and she had become sorta friendly. She could see he struggled when at bat and that got her asking him many questions. She had not been at the afternoon game with the *MS Mockingbirds* but she had heard he sent a spinner far into space and that they had won. Sparepart's family were also Catholic and so she met him after church. They were arranging a pick-up game.

"Wow, congrats, looks like you guys had a really good game yesterday," she started off the conversation.

"Yes, ma'am, we won 5-4," he said, a bit shyly.

"Well, who do you play next Saturday?"

"Ughhh, I think the *Roosters* or the," he hesitated as Gail walked toward him.

"Right well, I'll try to get to the game. I know you only have a few more until the playoffs. Is it still possible for your guys to get in?"

Sparepart's eyes followed Gail as she walked by, and walked away, a slight smile on her face as she looked back over her shoulder at him. He blushed.

"Ughhh, yes, ma'am, we have to win the next three games in a row."

"OK, then go winnum!"

++

Sunday afternoon at 12:30pm and Astra, Beatrice, Percy, Nevaeh and Alcor were having lunch. They were waiting for the three grumpy sisters who were not as grumpy as they had once been.

"*Red, white & blue plate*," Astra ordered. The others went on and ordered, though they usually waited for each other. The sisters were over forty-five minutes late. Somthin' was up!

Astra looked for her cell, not something she used often, and called Whiplash.

"Hey," she had to shout, "whassup?"

"Girlfriend," Whiplash yelled back, "I'm at the hospital. Sparepart was hit in the wrist by a seventy-mph fastball in a pick- up game this morning after church and it is broken. They think surgery before they can cast it. Might need a plate or something. We won't be coming. Sorry I couldn't phone!"

"Oh, gosh," Astra was trying to finish the talk with her and tell the others what had happened. "I'll be right over." She hung up, inhaled the rest of her fried chicken and yams and de-café and headed for the car. Percy and Alcor went along. They were done eating. Beatrice took Nevaeh home. "Phone me," she said. "We will."

++

Moira was so excited to be on a winning team for a change. The *MS Mockingbirds* went home very unhappy, as they had hoped to secure the league lead again. Now they were tied for second. (They had rejected Moira during try-outs!)

There awaiting Moira near her dug-out was Trakayla who greeted her, and others, with a big hug.

"Girl, you were brilliant!" she shouted out over the din of excited shouts and cheering.

"Let's go getta burger?"

"OK, yea, I'm so hungry! Oh wait, let's see if the team is going to eat somewhere together and then you can come with us."

"Coach Dan, are we going together to eat? Do you know my cousin, a former *Hotdogs Rule* player, a great pitcher?"

"No, not today, but I'm very happy to meet your cousin. Hey, Ms. Trakayla. You have quite a record. It's a pleasure to meet you. You guys go off and eat. Practice, Tuesday afternoon, OK, slugger?"

Moira beamed from ear to ear. "You got it Coach." Off they went to *KINGDOMBURGERS* and caught up on lots of family and baseball business.

"Are you back here to stay?" Moira asked with great hope.

"Well for a little while. I'm at least here for your next three games and hoping my cheering will get the *Hotdogs Rule* into the play-offs."

"OK, if we win…you gotta stay," she playfully said to her cousin. "You gotta stay!"

++

Astra, Percy and Alcor got to the hospital and met up with Whiplash, Melodious and Sarahfinna. Thomas Junior was with Sparepart who was being prepped for surgery. His mom had stayed home with his two year old brother.

"I am so sorry," Astra began. "Do you guys need anything? We can go get some food for you?"

"Naw," Melodious said. "We'll go down to the cafeteria when he goes into surgery. Will you join us?"

"Of, course," Percy squeaked out and Alcor joined her.

"What actually happened?"

"Well, he went over to another boy's house with five or six guys. They said they were going to play catch and practice. When he didn't come home in time for lunch Thomas Junior called over to the boy's house at just about the minute the young pitcher threw his very fast ball for Sparepart to hit. Instead, it cracked onto the top of his left wrist and he hit the dust. The boy's mother phoned Thomas Junior and he rushed over to get him and here we are at the hospital."

There were no other people in the waiting room so they sat in chairs all next to one another. Thomas Junior came out and said the doctors thought the surgery would be about an hour or a little more unless they got in there and found more damage than they expected. They all went down to the cafeteria and waited.

++

Moira and Trakayla went to *KINGDOMBURGERS* and ate a Bruno-Big Burger and some of their famous sweet potato fries. Then they had a Frostyfull and kept talking. Moira's phone rang. Her face changed and Trakayla was concerned.

Whassup? she tried to signal, asking with scrunched up shoulders.

One minute, one minute, Moira silently indicated, raising her finger. She was having trouble hearing Chris tell her about Sparepart. Then she hung up.

"Well," she began quickly, "the guys were playing catch, then a bit of a pick-up game a few hours ago and a pitch broke Sparepart's left wrist and he's in surgery. May we go over to the hospital?"

"Of course," Trakayla said. They scooped up the rest of their cokes and Frostyfulls and headed for the car.

++

Thomas Junior was waiting with some anxiety for his son's surgery to be over. More and more folks from Sparepart's baseball world had come and were sitting and waiting with him. He'd been in there over an hour already.

It would be nearly another hour before his surgery was complete and he was in the recovery room. Dr. Ben came out and explained to Thomas Junior the good and bad news. He would stay in hospital for at least a week and then they would see what he needed.

The good news was he would likely be OK eventually. Dr. Ben had to put in a plate and Sparepart would need lots of physical therapy. The worst, of course, was his baseball career for a long while was over. All his team members looked aghast at one another. How would they get by without Sparepart? He was the team's sparkplug.

++

The next week passed slowly and included various folk going over to the hospital to visit Sparepart. He was beginning to feel a bit better and folks had drawn and written all over his cast. They brought him all kinds of snacks and drinks and his favorite after-the-game-drink of blue gatorade2. The team would face the *Roosters* on Saturday. He would still be in the hospital. Would they have a chance? They needed to win the last three games to get into the play-offs.

++

On Monday Astra had phoned Road-Post to find out where her parcel, containing the three movies, was. She had tried to track it on her computer but for some reason had no luck whatsoever. Only six days until Sunday afternoon for the double-header promised to the community. Folks felt a bit moldy anyway at Sparepart's accident and she didn't want to add to it. The woman in charge at Road-Post said she had no idea at all where the parcel was, or where it went wrong from the sports library at the University (only 547 miles away). Astra Fisic's heart sank. What to do now?

++

Percy was working over at '*the dogwood*' when the mail arrived and was stacked in the box. Bingo, who would believe this? There were Astra's movies at the bottom of the stack. They had been delivered to the science center instead of Astra's home. Perhaps they had been sitting there for a few days but here it was already Friday and she couldn't wait to phone Astra.

++

Sparepart was on his way home from hospital and hoping to be able to go to the movies on Sunday. Thomas Junior said they'd wait and see. Astra was so excited that the films had been found. She was on her way out the door to the *Roosters* game. They had to win. They did. 3-2. Sparepart was missed but they won that one for him! The following week they would play the *Bluebirds* and their last game would be the *MS Mockingbirds* again. Would they make the play-offs?

++

There were over 150 people gathered to watch the double- header with something special in between. Astra got up to tell folks about the movies and where the popcorn and hot dogs might be found. There was a stilled crowd looking forward to learning what the movies would be. Baseball was for everyone and so there were as many girls there as boys.

"The first film of the double-header is '*A LEAGUE OF THEIR OWN*' (1992), starring Tom Hanks and Geena Davis as Dottie Hinson. It is the story of the *Racine Belles* and the first professional baseball league for women (frequently called girls!). The chewing gum mogul Philip Wrigley supported the league and had the women pitching overhand by the 1948 season. There are women from this era admitted into the Baseball Hall of Fame since 1988. *Mrs. America*, Fredda Acker played for the South Bend Blue Soxs and was both pitcher and beauty queen.

In 1943, 280 women were invited to try out and sixty were chosen. The first spring training was in May, 1943, with salaries of those signed to clubs between $45-85 a week. Helena Rubenstein's Beauty Salon provided training in the area of femininity and the uniforms were designed by Mrs. Wrigley's art designer. The uniform was a one-piece short-skirted flared tunic (like field hockey players) with satin shorts, knee-high baseball socks and a baseball hat. Each city had its own colors and patch, though the uniforms were all the same. By 1945 there were over 450, 313 in attendance."

Folks cheered.

"Following that film I will be showing shorts of the 1947 *LL World Series,* the very first one. The *Maynard Midgets* of Williamsport, PA, beat the *Lock Haven All-Stars* of Lock Haven, PA, 16-7. Little League was founded in 1938 by Carl Stotz for his nephews." Folks clapped.

"And then the second film of this double-header will be *"42"* staring Chadwick Boseman as Jackie Robinson, along with Harrison Ford and Nicole Beharie, 2013. This film highlights the coming into the white major leagues of the first black player, Jackie Robinson in 1947. The first *LL World Series* of the same year was already integrated.

The Negro League was still in business but was waning as white teams saw the worth of black players and began, after Robinson's season, to sign them. In 1947, the *NY Cubans* of the National Negro League beat the *Cleveland Buckeyes* of the Negro American League 4-1 in the Negro World Series, with one tie called in the sixth inning for rain. Standing alongside and watching attentively was young Willie Mays soon to step out and play his first professional season at seventeen with the *Birmingham Black Barons* of the Negro American League who won the 1948 Negro World Series, 4-1 over the *Washington Homestead Greys* of the Negro National League."

Folks cheered and clapped. The lights went down and the house was silent as the first film began.

++

Coach Tony was keeping an eye on Sparepart but knew he would not be available for this up-coming season. Folks loved the films and they provided lots of food for thought and conversation. The *Hotdogs Rule* won the next game. Alas, they lost the final one to the *MS Mockingbirds 3-1,* yet again not making the playoffs. One thing about baseball, there's always next year. Baseball is a sort of failure sport…and so you have to know how to get over it rather quickly and move on! The kids were returning to school and the whole county was proud of their LL program. One day, Williamsport the old boys said, one day…

THE END

8

Astra Fisic and the Little Fishes and Loaves

Astra Fisic, the slightly retired astronomer, who wears a red hat, and her three friends were having breakfast at Thee Café one Sunday morning. They had discussed all the things they usually discuss when Astra Fisic began to tell them about her first night of volunteering at the soup kitchen in Nearby City.

"You know," she began, "there are a lot more hungry people than I thought. Why, when I went over to *Little Fishes & Loaves,* there were already about thirty people standing around in a line peacefully chatting with one another waiting for the door to open." Her listeners were locked in.

"Nearby City is only twenty-five miles away. We don't have any hungry people here," a shocked Whiplash interjected.

"Are you sure?" Astra asked. "Why have you ever been over to our food bank on a Thursday to see all the cars that pull up to receive boxes of food?"

"Well, no," she said.

"Maybe they just need to get a job and buy their own food?" asked Melodious.

"Maybe so, but many, if not most of them, are elderly types who are clearly not going to go back to work! And there are moms getting food for their children. What really bothered me were the families where the adults were working and they couldn't make it, even with their food stamps!"

Sarahfinna, Melodious and Whiplash, along with Alcor and Percy had joined Astra that Sunday morning for a tall-stack, eggs and blueberry syrup. And they drank coffee, coke and water. Nevaeh had stayed home with Beatrice.

"I was greeted by Elmer who was the director of the soup kitchen and he was so gracious and happy to have another helper. We went into the kitchen to meet all the volunteers for that night. They were from the *Churches Link* a group of downtown folks who were every-denomination and gathered to help the poor. The kitchen was open three nights a week and Tuesdays were their night.

The food smelled wonderful. There are so many jobs, so the volunteers come a couple of hours earlier. The bathrooms were cleaned and sparkling and the floor of the very large old office building had recently been painted a bright red, the walls a soft off pink that was very soothing. Over in the corner was a whole area for children. On the floor, they had painted many games and little tables and chair were set for them.

Some bring food already cooked at home but Elmer prefers it cooked there. The little kitchen was a bit crowded but the volunteers seemed not to worry. "I was given a simple job to start off with," she continued, "stacking plates, putting out trays, and making up napkin sets with the colorful designs showing."

Her listeners were interested, were eating, and were wanting to know what happened next.

"I made up 100 sets. Elmer told me there would be at least that many and the majority would be little families with hungry children. Some would be single men or women from the streets. Some would be elderly who just liked to come over from the group home to sit and chat and eat with other folks."

Percy had been using her screen and looking up hunger statistics for Mississippi. She was amazed. "These people must be hidden somewhere," she said. "I don't see them here! Especially out here in the country."

"Right," Astra said, "notice, they can't afford our Sunday breakfast."

They all looked over at one another. "Maybe we need to do something as well?" Sarahfinna asked.

"Well, let me tell you more about what happened that night and that might help us make some decisions!" Astra Fisic continued.

"After that job, Elmer asked me to take rolls out of packages and put on platters, and then I arranged the packaged deserts on another table. The cut cakes, pies, and other donated goodies would be coming. And they sure did!

The job I found most difficult to start with was sitting with Homer, Gladys and their three (very dirty) children Teeny, Tiny & Tom. Yes, I know, but that's what they called them. Their clothing was smelly, their personal grooming was horrid, and most of them had no teeth. The girls were eleven and nine, and Tom was eight months. Homer and Gladys were in their late thirties, he had no work, and they had no place to live."

Folks listened but were dubious. They mumbled a bit under their breath that there was no reason for homelessness if people would just get themselves together. They also talked about how many people 'cheat the system'.

"I know what you might be thinking, because I have thought it myself," Astra went on. "Listen, everyone has a story and some of them are tragic. In fact, there are many tragic stories right around us. We saw that when we opened '*the dogwood*' and how many people keep coming out to the lectures and the classes just to be with other people as well as eat a bit! You don't really think all those folks are *that* into science, do you?"

They shook their heads no.

"Elmer called me over and showed me the way to the showers and clean clothes. I was amazed at the huge rooms set aside. The *Little Fishes and Loaves* folks really had this down to a T.

Two shower rooms had been purpose built. The women's also had provision for children and babies and the men's had stacks of towels, shavers, and clothes. Elmer explained that if people were able, even if only once a week, to get clean and feel their hair squeak and look at their children and see them in a new dress or some clean jeans, they would be able to re-connect with their lives. As he talked it made sense to me. So he invited me to go over and talk to Homer and Gladys and see if they might be interested in washing up before dinner. And I did just that."

"It was a little difficult to begin, I found, as I didn't want to embarrass them or make them feel like they *had* to wash up or they would get no food. But they were very gracious and looked forward to seeing what I was talking about. It was their first visit to *Little Fishes and Loaves*."

++

Beatrice and Nevaeh were getting ready to go to Church. They were Methodists and Nevaeh loved her Sunday School class. "What will learn to day? Jeezus?" she asked. She was growing fast and was talking as best she could.

"Don't know, but you will listen, and sing and pray, right?"

"Yes, ma'am," she blurted out. "Where'z suster, Percy?"

"She went over to Thee Café with the Sunday breakfast ladies."

"Why we no go? I hongree!"

"Well, you already ate and I wanted to stay with you!" Beatrice hugged her. "We need to finish getting ready to go to Church."

++

Astra had so much more to tell them and they wanted to know the outcome of Gladys and Homer and Teeny, Tiny and Tom.

"I had taken some food over to their table and it was gone before I could tell them that this was not the meal but just a snack. Then I asked Gladys if I might have a private word with her. Homer took Tom, and the girls went over to the play area. Gladys and I walked back to the shower room and her eyes filled with tears. She was so surprised but more than that, she knew her family felt horrible and wanted to find a place to live. No one, she told me, would even think about renting to them, as they were so dirty. We went through all the clean clothes that might fit the girls and found some very cool jeans and tops for her. There was a box with shampoos, conditioners, body gels, tampons or pads, deodorants, shavers, powders, bits of make-up, and well, all sorts of creams. Toothbrushes, mouthwash and even floss was there. There were also nail files, clippers, razors and scissors. It was hard to imagine anything missing. Stacks of clean soft colorful towels, washcloths, diapers and packages of new little panties for the girls. Gladys was so excited. The clothes were hardly-used-recycled and all the stuff for the shower was brand new and Gladys was free to take a little bag full with her when they left.

You know, I don't think I've ever seen pure joy but I was very close that night. Gladys could not stop smiling."

"I am so grateful," she kept saying. "I am so grateful. The last place we stopped made us feel like heathens and dirty slobs. I am so grateful just to feel that folks aren't looking down on us because we've had some hardship."

"I burst into tears, yes, your old Astra, burst into tears of joy and dismay and Gladys and I hugged, dirt and all."

++

The preacher moved over to the little podium and asked the well over 100 folks to hush that she might offer a prayer of thanksgiving:

> *"Lord, how fortunate we are to have friends and family. How fortunate we are to have food and clothes, and even the opportunity to help one another. We ask Your blessing tonight on us all that we may never forget that You are our provider and we have but a few little fish and loaves to share. Help us to learn to serve one another no matter our situation. Help us to give what we can, receive what we need, and allow You to fill our hearts with joy and thanksgiving. May we ever be grateful for all that comes our way. Let us all say AMEN!*

"That was the most sincere *Amen* I'd ever heard. I looked over at the squeaky-est clean Teeny, Tiny and Tom, Homer and Gladys. They were exhausted and needed a place to sleep for the night."

Over in one corner was a little office-sorta-space where families or folks could go and find other supports they needed. Homer went over and he was given a card to present to Bill for a week's stay at the Bethlehem Shelter some three blocks away. Elmer told him to take one of the sports bags and fill it with clothes and necessities for his family. He mentioned they would only have one meal a day at the shelter so to take breakfast type food and to be sure and come back Thursday night. Homer was full of thank you's."

"So what *was* their story?" Whiplash wanted to know.

"Homer had been in prison, just after Teeny was born. He was released when she was seven, and they had a nice little apartment. Gladys had been working at a fast-food place and wasn't making very much money. The rent came due, once, then, twice and then they were thrown out. Then came Tiny. The after-prison program Homer was involved with didn't really help much. They had nowhere to go. Then came Tom.

So they decided to come south hoping that we might have something for them. Homer had driven a truck for many years before going to prison and so he tried to get a job. His felony got in his way. Finally, he met an old man with a pick-up who needed some work done around his farm. He said they could sleep in the barn and the work would take about two weeks. He would pay them and they could have the truck. Homer and Gladys did the work and the children played around the farm, chasing the chickens and talking to the old horse named Ringthebell.

It didn't exactly go the way they'd hoped but the man did pay them and they loaded up in the truck and started for Mississippi. When they got into Arkansas they were pulled over by the State Troopers and Homer was arrested for stealing the truck. He had forgotten to get the papers and his family was stranded again. The local Arkansas police were kind enough to track down the old man and in a day or two it was settled and Homer was set free. He was scared, sure he was going back to prison, but he said that God had sent His angel to protect them, and he surely did. Gladys had the money from their work and found a motel and some food."

"Those police didn't have to do that, after all the trouble Homer had seen!" Melodious said.

"Of course, they did," Astra said. "He had a credible story no matter his past!"

"Anyway, they kept coming to Mississippi and found an old smoke-filled motel on the edge of a tiny town in the delta. Really, it was disgusting as Gladys told the story, but it was a bed or two (with bugs) and they could rest from their journey. They had no idea where to go, as they'd never been to Mississippi before. The truck was still running but loved to drink that gas and their money was running out. They got as far as Nearby City and the truck broke down and wasn't going to be fixed. Homer sold what was left of it and that was all the money they had. They found another ghastly motel and stayed for a few days. They were able to eat some but the kids were having a hard time. The baby seemed sick. This time, though, they had to try to find a place to squat on a street in Nearby City. That was about three weeks ago and now we meet them here at *Little Fishes and Loaves*."

"Sounds like they are still needin' a lot," Percy remarked. "I remember when Nevaeh and I were doin' the bus thing commin' south. It were really hard. She was so tiny and I didn't have no money sometimes to feed her. She needed what Tom needs now. I wish we could help!"

"Well, they are staying over at the Bethlehem Shelter on 2nd street in Nearby City. Maybe a couple of us could go over and visit?"

"Yea, I'll come," Percy was first and then Melodious and Alcor who had been silent through it all. "When are we going?"

"I'm game to go anytime. I think they have to vacate the premises during the day and then they get back in around 4 for their meal and Church. We could get there about 4 today and at least take them out for dinner…maybe *KINGDOMBURGERS*?"

"Yes," they chimed in together. "What time do we leave and…"

"OK, how about I pick up Percy and then get Alcor. Then we'll swing by your place, Melodious? OK? How about leaving town around three so we can be sure to find them around four?"

Folks agreed.

++

The trip over to Bethlehem Shelter went without a hitch. The women enjoyed being together and they had all been to Church that morning. When they arrived, Astra went to the door and asked for the family. The person in charge said they weren't there anymore as the baby had gotten sick and they left in a hurry for the hospital. The girls loaded up and went to Nearby City Memorial.

Hospitals are always busy places no matter the time of day. Astra inquired as to where the pediatrics might be and off they set. When they arrived Astra saw Gladys and Homer sitting with their faces fallen into their hands weeping. Teeny and Tiny came over and grabbed Melodious and Percy around the legs. Teeny talked, mixed with tears, "Tom died about an hour ago. They said he'd been bitten by some bug and the infection killed him because he wasn't very strong from not eating enough." She continued to cry, hugging Tiny. "It makes me sooooo mad!"

Astra and the rest stood still. She moved over and took the chair on the other side of Gladys. "Oh, my, oh my," she mumbled. "Come here," and she wrapped herself around Gladys.

Dr. Carmine came over and wanted to talk with them. She said how sorry she was. "Do you want these folks to stay with you or do you want to come to my office alone?"

"They can stay." Homer said.

They circled the chairs and Dr. Carmine explained what she thought had happened and why they could not do anything to stop it. She wanted them to be able to go in and hold Tom again so she had a nurse clean him all up, taking away the tubes. It was important that they could have special time with him. Then they would have to decide about burial. She explained it would cost money they didn't have, but there was charity money at the hospital and she would have a social worker come over in a few minutes to help with that and discuss with them other needs. Did they understand? Yes.

Homer shook her hand and thanked her for all her help. Then she suggested the family go together into the little room she'd prepared with Tom's little body. Off they went.

Astra and the women stayed for about half an hour and the family came back out, weeping. Gladys said he looked very peaceful and she had let him go to God. Homer smiled and agreed. "I'll missum', my boy, I'll missum'." The girls were not weeping but in a state of shock. They still had two days left at the shelter so Astra tried to phone and see what to do. The man in charge said they could come for the two days but he would not be able to give them another week as she'd asked for. There are just too many people. Astra was not well pleased.

"Their child just died," she emphasized. Would you please see if you can't arrange something?" The family hadn't eaten for a day or two as they'd been at the hospital with Tom and had no money. Astra and the women took them out and they ate and ate.

Astra turned to Gladys and asked what they could do.

"Well, I can leave Tom's body here until we decide. I think we'll have him cremated but I'm not sure where to bury his ashes."

"Maybe we can help with that," Melodious said. "We have some plots out on the edge of our farm. If you like it I'm sure my sisters and I would be pleased to have your little Tom there."

Gladys looked over at Homer and they nodded. "That would be so very fine," he said softly. "So very fine for our little son."

++

A few days later after all the business was taken care of, including getting another *two* weeks at Bethlehem Shelter, they had a little memorial service for Tom, eight months old, out at the farm of Melodious, Sarahfinna and Whiplash. Beatrice and Nevaeh came along, and Alcor attended. The Rev. Karen from *Churches Link* came over and did a lovely little service. After the home-going, they all went out to eat.

++

"It's hard for me to understand how some folks believe that other folks just have to get it together and their problems would be solved. Why little Tom couldn't do anything about his miseries!" Alcor said, tears in her eyes. It had been about a week since the funeral and they had stayed close to Gladys and her family.

++

Elmer over at *Little Fishes and Loaves* had found Homer a small part-time job that included a one- bedroom apartment. They were a bit stuffed up, as Tiny said, but they were together and dad was working. The girls were enrolled in school (where they got breakfast and lunch and a backpack over the weekend) and Gladys began looking for a job at the fast-food place. She got it and it included bringing home one meal a day. Three nights a week for a while the family went over to *Little Fishes and Loaves* for supper, met Astra and her friends at least once a week, and the kids met friends to play with. Elmer was always on the lookout for a better job for either of them, but for now they were doing OK. They found Rev. Karen's Church and went there. The Sunday reading was this:

> *"Be compassionate as Your Father is compassionate. Do not judge, and you will not be judged yourselves; do not condemn, and you will not be condemned yourselves; grant pardon, and you will be pardoned. Give and there will be gifts for you: a full measure, pressed down, shaken together, and running over, will be poured into your lap; because the amount you measure out is the amount you will be given back."* (Lk6:36-38)

Homer helped take up the offering and Gladys sang in the choir. The girls were in their classes and they were all going to meet Astra Fisic and her three friends at Thee Café for lunch after Church. What a blessing.

THE END

9

Astra Fisic and the Dogwood Marble Jubilee

Astra and her friends were preparing for the Marble Jubilee to be held near '*the dogwood*' in three months' time. Seems there hadn't been many tournaments, or none she could find advertised (except that one fifty years ago) so they decided at '*the dogwood*' to bring back a game from a quieter era…or so they thought.

The sun shone and it was the beginning of summer in MS. Yes, it would get hotter but just now it was glorious. Why you could even have an open window in your room and await the sweet breeze that blew through. No need for A/C yet. Beatrice, Percy and Neveah, were glad school was out and intended to get out their marbles and see what they might use for the up-coming Jubilee. Nevaeh was quite keen and knew she could win if she tried hard enough. Percy and Beatrice were not competing. Beatrice was the Chairperson of the Jubilee and Percy agreed to be her go-fer.

Max and Sherrilynn were planning to enter the Tween and Teen divisions and her grandfather Mr. Spencer was heading the list of Seniors and believe it or not he was a champ from fifty years ago and intended to win the *Silver Cup* and *HandBlown Glass Orb*. Not only did he have to win his Senior division he had to win the play-offs which included all divisional winners: Kids 6-10, Tweens 11-12, Teens 13-15, Young Adults 16-20, Adults 21+ and the Senior Division 55+. The winner of the single elimination Final would take home the *Silver Cup* with the *HandBlown Glass Orb*.

Mr. Spencer, or Bagger, as he was most often called, was a Korean Vet and had played marbles all his life. He said he even had a pocketful when he was at war! His grandfather, Pop-Paw Bagger, gave him his first bag of cleareys and peewees when he was only five figuring the lad had gotten over eating everything in sight and his mother JaniceLei wouldn't mind! Well that set him off on a marble collecting life. His brother Boner (that's bone-r) was three years younger and Pop-Paw would be gone by the time he would want marbles too. He did however, love marbles and Bagger helped him start his collection; then they competed so many times they could not count that high. Bagger could remember the first time he opened the bag and those glowing little treasures poured out onto the carpet of the shed. Pop-Paw Bagger and he sat down on the floor for well over two hours and marveled at the colors and designs. He imagined they'd fallen from the planets or were very expensive jewels. Pop-Paw brought some of his smokies, milkies, and purees to show Bagger and they sat in silence turning and lifting each one into the light pouring through the window in the shed. Pop-Paw also had his taws (shooters) with their cat-eyes center and some rainbows for Bagger to see. He was not sure he was going to let him play with them yet but he did let him choose a taw for his own. Bagger looked very carefully at all the beautiful shooters on the carpet and just could not decide.

"Well," said Pop-Paw, "if you hold it like this and turn it like that, and roll it around a bit, each one, even though they are all round, has a slightly different feel. Now you try." Bagger picked up each of the twelve shooters, one at a time, and rolled them around in his tiny hand and looked up into the sunlight and finally chose. Even as a small child he had a lot of patience and willingly waited for things to emerge. He'd pick the right shooter.

"This one, Pop-Paw," he said with some excitement. "this one's just right!"

Pop-Paw Bagger had a grin all over his face. How could he tell the boy it was *his* very favorite taw, his alley (most expensive) worth a lot of money? Maybe he should have left it out of the choosing pile? He never told Bagger his secret. To let go, even to a favored grandson, ones taw was a huge sacrifice. Why Pop-Paw Bagger had had that marble for nearly thirty-five years, though it glowed as if he'd just bought it. He won many a game and competition with that shooter. What would he have used in the *DOGWOOD MARBLE JUBILEE*? Bagger, on the other hand, was going to use it in his Senior division play! That alley must be nearly 100 years old.

Max and Sherrilynn were cousins about three years apart, Sherrilynn being the older at fifteen (her Granni being JaniceLei) and Max twelve (his Gramps being Boner). They were going to enter the Marble Jubilee at '*the dogwood*'. They practiced all summer to be ready. It took some sorting and polishing as well as flicking and learning to keep those knuckles down. Sherrilynn preferred milkies and rainbows and her big taw was as clear as glass could be. She kept it polished and perched on a ring-stand living in her bedroom to avoid all fingerprints. She figured it was also her alley. Max, on the other hand, favored cleareys and purees and had a spectacular turquoise swirl, a clear glass shooter about the size of a quarter. He had saved up for a long time to buy it and his Gramps, Boner, had helped him. He had had it for over two years and had never used it in a tournament setting, only for local games. He preferred playing on a carpet rather than in the dirt, but his taw was ready for anything.

++

It was an unusually beautiful morning, a cool breeze would fool you if you didn't know better! It was gonna be hot, and soon, but for the moment it was perfect. Astra Fisic, the slightly retired astronomer who almost always wears a red hat, was reading one of her astronomy books when Percy and Beatrice bounced into her den. The three used-to-be-grumpy sisters had been there for about half an hour.

"There's only one month left until the Marble Jubilee," Beatrice began at speed. "We need to do so much work over at 'the dogwood' to get ready." Percy stood by feeling very happy that she had finally earned her AA Degree in May (Advanced Business Administration) and her little sister Nevaeh finished second grade. (That's another whole story). She had served for a while as the secretary at 'the dogwood' but was now differently employed with a company that required some travel.

"I saw the most amazing tourney," she began, " when I was up in Ohio. I have to go there once in a while for my new job and I was so excited. I was in this tiny town on the River and these folks had gathered on a Saturday morning for their annual Championship Ring Game."

Astra Fisic and Beatrice were intensely interested. The sisters set up in their chairs.

"A gentleman in a very tall hat appeared and began kinda shouting or singing a message to the people, like to the whole village. There musta been over 150 people there, all sorts of people and they all paid attention to him. I think it went something like:

> 'Hear ye, hear ye, the annual Mossgreen CHAMPIONSHIP
> Marble Tournament and Children's Match is about to
> begin. Mibsters git yer kimmies at the ready.' He took off
> his hat and bowed, and then disappeared into the crowd
> as the noise level exploded. Folks were cheering and
> looking for their assigned circle. Music blared from one

end of the field to the other down to the three circles set up for the Children's Match. I wished Nevaeh had been able to be there because she's very big into marbles, sure she is going to win the *Silver Cup* and *HandBlown Glass Orb*!"

Percy breathed. So did Beatrice and Astra. "So the whole point I'm trying to make is there's lots of work to do this month before September 7, Labor Day and the Jubilee." Beatrice was clear and finished. They agreed.

"Let's go to lunch at Thee Café," Astra suggested. "On the *red-white-and blue-plate* today is mac 'n cheese, grilled pork chop and squash, chocolate pound-cake with choc sauce. Oh, don't forget the sweet tea. Actually, I'm on unsweet at the moment! Whaddya think? I'm buying!" They agreed. Off they went, all in separate cars. They only had to travel some four blocks and would you think they could have gone together? Not really. The three sisters were, well, portly, except one who was just plain fat. Astra was not. Lunch was a delight as usual, though Astra had begun to think about how she and her friends might do a make-over of Thee Café . Little paint here and there, fixing the chairs, why even having an art contest…ok, ok, one thing at a time!

++

Astra showed up on Sunday, as usual, at Thee Café for breakfast before Church. Melodious, Sarafina and Whiplash were in attendance and were looking for her. Late again? They'd been friends so long that they knew each other's patterns. The three, who started out as rather grumpy sisters, weren't that grumpy anymore. They had learned some patience, and had begun to bring something interesting to the table themselves for discussion, not always waiting on Astra to produce. Melodious (who is tone-deaf and dearly loves to sing) brought a piece of new music, not sure if she wrote it, anyway, for them to listen to on her phone. They did and the only problem was Melodious trying to sing along. "Isn't that the most beautiful piece you've ever heard?" she inquired. Astra, Sarafina and Whiplash all looked at each other, grinned, and said, in unison, "Of course! Bless yer heart!" Then they laughed so loud Kisha heard them away back in the kitchen and came to check out the commotion. They couldn't keep from laughing but they did try.

Whiplash began to speak, "Hahah really? I mean really? Where did it...hahahaha...come from? " She looked lovingly into her sister's eyes and Melodious, who by now had put on her headset, didn't hear...she did smile back. She was a goner, off into her ethereal music cloud.

Astra and the sisters finished their breakfast and then needed to talk about the Jubilee. They frequently volunteered for various things in the community and they thought this would not be too strenuous and lotsa fun. After their brief conversation folks happened off to a Church of some flavor.

++

It was Tuesday and Astra's favorite day to go to the library. There she visited with Olive and Crystal, her assistant. Crystal's family originally came from Jamaica but she had been born in MS. Today she was looking for rules, rules for the Marble Jubilee. She thought she knew the basics and that if they could find a game or two that would be enough. There are so many marble games. They chose the Ring Game, the one Percy had mentioned, and she copied a few pages. She decided to stop over at Beatrice's to check it out. Nevaeh wasn't home from day-camp yet and Percy was at work. She and Beatrice had a little snack, well actually a big snack, of Red Velvet cake with cream cheese and ice cream that Percy had made. Beatrice had been trying to get her to cook more but to no avail. The treat was delish and they continued chatting with a coffee. Maybe Percy was better at baking?

"I've found the basic rules for the game," Astra said. "Wanna look and see if it will be sufficient for the Jubilee? Really they are the simple ones folks have been using but they are here in the Official Rule Book just to be sure."

Beatrice did just that and they agreed they would do nicely. Simple and straight forward, everyone could understand. 'The Ring Game'. The age categories seemed fair. The rings for Kids and Young Adults would be five foot and all Adults and Seniors would compete in the full six foot ring. To select who would go first in each game the youngest would have to be two feet away from the edge, next group four feet away, and adults would be the full ten feet away. You could shoot or roll your marbles (the *kimmies*) and the closest to the center would go first. Easy enough to chalk a little line where they had to shoot from. The circle for the Final would be four and a half to accommodate the youngest and still not make it that easy for the oldest. Astra and Beatrice were finished for the day, though they weren't finished by any means.

"We need to select the prizes (besides the *Silver Cup* and *HandBlown Glass Orb*) for each divisional winner," said Beatrice. "I think Whiplash and JasonMa are on that team. We also need players, referees, and judges T-shirts."

"Why don't you look and see what you think might work and I'll do the same and we'll meet again next Tues?" Astra gathered up her satchel, her red hat and headed off home. "Tell the girls I said hey!"

"Will do."

++

Sherrilynn and Max had begun to practice in earnest in the early summer. They had registered at the '*the dogwood*', each paying their $5, receiving back a welcome and the rules. The little leaflet also listed the age categories and the prizes. They read it with excitement, rolling their marbles around in their hands.

"Let's see," began Sherrilynn, 'you'll be in the Tween group and I'll be in the Teen. That's good. We don't have to compete, except for the *Silver Cup* and *HandBlown Glass Orb*."

Max just laughed. "You think *you'll* win? Really?"

"Well, I have as good a chance as anyone else. Don't you think?"

Max was silent. He knew better than to argue with his cousin continuing his smile as he rolled his taw in his hand. Maybe *I* could win, he thought, just maybe. He set off to the practice circle his dad had drawn them in the dirt behind their house. This circle was about four foot and the line outside the circle about three feet away. He made an 'X' of kimmies in the middle, got out his turquoise swirl taw and flicked it full across while trying to hold his knuckles to the ground. That was the hardest part and was where you could foul the most. Sherilynn practiced alone but they needed each other for the competition so they played friendlies. She always wanted to play keepsies but he never did, so afraid he might lose his best taw. She wanted it and he wasn't giving it up for anything!

++

Achariya Seng (they call her 'Knock') came by the library and spoke with Crystal about the Jubilee. She originally came from Cambodia sometime in the 70's when she was a child. Through a series of various foster families, she ended up in MS and has lived here since. As the Town Clerk, Knock was concerned about the structures of the Jubilee…tables, chairs, shade, water, etc. Her Clerk's office had received permission from the Mayor to do some of the copying and advertisement as well as the registration leaflets.

"We need to decide where the watchers will watch and the mibsters will sit and await their turns," said Knock. "I'm a bit concerned with the Children's circle." Crystal brought out a sort of an industrial map of the whole area showing play sites. She and Knock spent two hours going over it and deciding times, spaces, and events. "I think we've just about got it together," she grinned happily. Knock agreed. "Now we need to meet with Astra, Beatrice, and what's that man's name....ugh..."

"Oh, you mean Steven? What do they call him? Stringbean?" Knock said in a hushed sort of library voice. "We need to be sure the chalk for the rings is on hand and I think he knows where to find it and we need to be sure all the prizes are in. I'll check with JasonMa."

"Yea, that's right. He's supposed to be building, or finding the bleachers, chairs, etc. We also need a table for the prizes and another long one for the judges and referees. Let's go see if Astra knows where he is and/or what he's already done." They set off, leaving the library to Olive.

++

It was lunchtime at the old Thee Café and the *red-white-and-blue plate* was ham steak, green beans, cornbread, and blueberry cobbler. Of course, sweet or unsweet tea went along with the $5 special. Astra was with her friend Nevaeh who was having a cheeseburger and strawberry *Fanta*. They had been friends for about seven years. That's another story but just for now they had lots to share.

"I'm going to enter the Jubilee marble thing," she sorta whispered to Astra. "I want to win, especially cuz I love that Orb thingy. I'm saving up my $5. I already have $2.27!"

"Well, well," Astra popped back with a wide grin. "I think you have as good a chance as anyone! I'm not sure how it works but I know if you win the Kids division you'll get a twelve pack of *grasshopper boulders* for the prize. You know the yellowish green ones with the black swirls? I think boulders are about one inch big. Do you already have some?" Nevaeh sat back and tried to imagine her boulders. She had quite a few and enjoyed using them. "Naw, I don't have that color so that would be good. What are the other prizes?"

Astra took out her long paper and began reading: "Senior Division, a six pack of 7/8" *cobbles* in various colors and patterns with floral, swirl, feathered, and foil. Adults, *asteroid jumbos*. They are 1 3/8", opaque white with specks of blue and green. They are iridized to be extra shiny. I think there are three in the pack."

Nevaeh's eyes widened. "I want some of those," she chirped. "What are the rest?"

Astra continued. "Well, the Tweens win two inch *toebreakers*, a three pack, of Bengal tiger design, that's orange with black swirls. Let's see the Teens winner will get a three pack of 7/8" *earth marbles*. All are transparent with the earth's land formations printed into one. The other one has a peace sign and the third the word *peace*. That's sounds beautiful!"

Astra kept on. "The last is the Young Adults and the winner will receive genuine Japanese *cat's-eyes*, a twelve pack. Wow! That's a lot of winners and lots of prizes." Astra did have to wonder though, who would win the *Silver Cup* and *HandBlown Glass Orb*. There would also be a Runner-Up prize. She could not wait to see the Orb; should be in the post any time soon.

Nevaeh was tuckered out just trying to listen to all that. "I need to finish my burger and go home," she said very matter- of- fact-ly. "Mama Beatrice will be looking for me!" Astra agreed, they finished lunch and packed up their stuff. "Before we go though I want to show you this toebreaker Percy gave me for my last birthday. It is a vintage Mill-e-fiori (it sorta stuck on her tongue). That means 'a thousand flowers'. I'd like to know how it was made!" They carefully held the 1" marble and gazed in awe at its beauty. The artistry of the glass blower, a master gaffer, was astounding, so many colors and flowers. Clearly, it was time to set off. "Maybe one day you'll get the chance to see how marbles and orbs are made!" Nevaeh smiled and tucked that under her hat. "I hope you enter and do very well and mostly have some fun. Maybe the other nine year olds will be kids you know? Oh, here's twenty-five cents toward your registration fee." Astra smiled and Nevaeh gratefully took the quarter.

"Remember the coin collection? (That's another story too)." Nevaeh asked. Astra beamed. "You remember that all the way back to where you were so new and so young?"

"Yup, I still collect coins I find interesting. One day I'll show ya. Percy gave me that big dollar coin with the Shoshone woman on it. Since then I've also found a Susan B. Anthony $1. In 2020 they are supposed to be making a $20 bill with Harriet Tubman on it…replacing Jackson. Do you think that will even happen?" Astra did wonder.

++

Only one week left until the Jubilee. Nevaeh was fifth in the registration line when she took in her $5, waiting as the excitement grew. People from various parts of the County were welcome. No one out of County could compete but could certainly pay the $2.50 to get in and watch, shop or become a vendor, renting a table for the day and selling their wares.

Marbles and all stuff pertaining to marbles were available. There was a variety of food, banners, jewelry, and the like. Homemade ice cream, some made on the spot, popsicles and sno-cones would be in evidence. It would become a large end-of-summer fair really by the time Labor Day rolled around. Based on the registration (soon to close) there would be two Senior circles and one each Adult, Young Adult, Teen, Tween, and Kids circle. The Senior circle would play off with a game of *marrididdles*, that's of homemade marbles made of clay by *Jack'sPottery* over in the Delta. The semi-Final, with the three pairs of winners of each division, would be held around 2:30pm and the Final at 4pm to decide the winner of the *Silver Cup* and *HandBlown Glass Orb*. The circles would be scattered around the grounds (the back of the High School where the baseball fields are). Some friends of Astra's had made wonderful signs to make it so easy for mibsters and onlookers to find their way. The Championship Circle, however, was in a very special place central to the grounds and there was plenty of room for folks to gather round it to see the mibsters compete.

++

It was Thursday night and the final meeting of the Dogwood Marble Jubilee Committee had come to order. Beatrice went over a few small housekeeping details and then each little team gave their reports. The *Silver Cup* (properly engraved except the winner's name) had come but the *HandBlown Glass Orb* had not. This was not a happy moment.

"Where does it have to come from?" Stringbean asked.

"I think it was to be made in a little art studio of designer glass in Alabama. Not that far away," replied Knock.

"What's the plan?" he asked.

"Not sure" she responded, "but we have to have delivery either tomorrow or Saturday at the latest. Labor Day is Monday and it's the Jubilee and there's no mail delivery!"

The rest of the meeting went well. All teams reporting and all things go, except part of the big prize. Stringbean went to see Beatrice.

"What if I drive over to Alabama and get the thing?"

"Well, you could but we'd need to phone first. Maybe something happened in the post or it's not finished, or they never got our order or..." Beatrice babbled with nerves.

"OK, you let me know and I will do what works." Stringbean left and Beatrice tried to find the phone number of *HandBlown Glass Designs*, near Tuscaloosa. She looked everywhere and it seemed unfindable. Someone must have it or I'll just call directory assistance. I hate to pay all that money for them to look it up for me. There we are she mused. Within the hour, she had talked to a Mexican woman artist at the studio and it was clear she did not know what Beatrice was talking about! Sonia agreed to contact Mark who was the blower of the orbs, consult him and get right back to them. She clearly understood their problem, but not what had happened to *their* Orb. Beatrice sat down, head in hands and prayed. A few tears of frustration filled her eyes.

Percy came in from work and caught her uncharacteristically blue. "What's up, Mama Beatrice?" She gently explained what she knew and they both sat a bit amused and a bit down. "I suspect it was never ordered," Beatrice said. "I'll hope to talk to the glass artist soon. Maybe he has something else on hand? I don't want to embarrass our team who may have overlooked it. " That was a hope denied as the glass blower did not phone until late Saturday afternoon. He'd been away doing an exhibition and just returned. No, he had not received an order, but maybe he had a suggestion. He did. She loved it.

++

Sunday morning was of course Thee Café and the usual suspects were in attendance. Tall stacks with blueberry syrup all round and the talk of the town was the Jubilee the next day. Melodious, Sarafina, and Whiplash had come in and ordered only to find their favorite booth filled by others. That was never a happiness. Since the general mood around was one of joy they realized they needn't muck it up with complaining. Astra, Beatrice, Nevaeh, and Percy were coming through the door looking for a place. Stringbean, Olive, Crystal, Knock and about ten others gathered around to hear any news. (There were thirty-two booths and ten tables; seemed enough room for everyone!)

Beatrice, since she was the Chairperson, stood up as others munched through their breakfasts. "I have some bad news and some good news," she began. "Whoever was supposed to order the Orb for the grand-prize didn't do it and so we do not have one." Groans filled Thee Café and a very red-faced Whiplash looked around. She acted as if she wanted to melt away somewhere under a table. She is, as you remember quite portly, so that was not an option. She sat for a minute and listened to Beatrice, and looked around for JasonMa who was not there.

"However, I have contacted Mark the glass blower and he is going to bring his exhibition RV tomorrow to the Jubilee and demonstrate how it's done! Right here for all to see! He also agreed to show us how to make a marble from scratch. We'll all learn lots. Now how does that sound?" Folks burst out into excited clappin', hootin', whistlin', shoutin', and well just jumpin' for joy.

"That's a great answer. A win-win", Stringbean shouted out. "Now we'll have what we need for the Champion and the rest of us will have learned more than we ever would have! You know, sometimes unexpected consequences do work out for the good."

"Yes," Beatrice called back, "He seems a very sweet person and we look forward to seeing his work firsthand. After the 4pm Championship Final round we'll know the winners of the Grand Prize and Runner-Up. The competition games will begin around 1pm so we hope he will be able to do his exhibition around 11am. That will give everybody a chance to see some of how it works."

Folks agreed, smiled, picked up their stuff and went off to Church. Well, all except Whiplash who needed to talk to Beatrice. She waited until everyone was gone and then sat down near her friend.

"Oh, I can't believe I let everybody down," she began. "I'm so embarrassed. I wrote the order we'd agreed to, you know size, colors, etc. down on a piece of toilet paper. That was all I had. I must have flushed it and then it totally slipped my mind! I am so sorry." Beatrice put her arm around her shoulders and squeezed a bit. "No worries, my friend things happen. I think it worked out even better to have him come over and finish blowing it right here. Don't you? I never knew his studio had an exhibition RV or we might have invited him from the beginning."

Whiplash had filled up with tears and her face was still red, and though she accepted Beatrice's forgiveness, she still felt a bit moldy. "I'm still just so sorry. Are you going to tell everyone?" She hung her head and her chin plopped onto her breast.

"Should I?"

"Well, it doesn't really matter now because my team knows I failed," she concluded. "I wish I'd paid more attention to JasonMa. He probably reminded me at some point and I just went off as usual doing my own thing." Beatrice put her finger under Whiplash's chin and raised her face up. "Well if anyone who needs to know asks, we'll tell them. Otherwise, we will just conclude that this oversight is <u>over</u>. Bless yer little heart." (That said with empathy not criticism!). Beatrice smiled, consulted her watch, and set off for Church. She surely needed Church today. She was tired and a bit miffed that things weren't going more smoothly. She needed to hand it over. It was not about her. Whiplash remained behind and had a coffee.

++

They'd all be gathering again in the afternoon at the site to begin the set-up for tomorrow. Vendors and players could come in and familiarize themselves with what they needed or wanted for their booth, and see where the rings would be. Labor Day the grounds would open around 7am. The registration desk would be front and center for all the mibsters to get their numbers and directions to their place of competition.

Despite the fact that it was a happy town, when lots of folks get together to pull off something this big there might be controversy, complaining, and even tears. The Sunday afternoon setting up of the circles shows my point. Stringbean and Boner had been asked to draw the circles (with the same white chalky stuff as the baseball field's lines) to the size required for each age group and to make sure that the big circle for the Final was drawn properly, with the shooting lines clear. For some reason James, who was not on that team, approached and began to question their work. Next thing Boner knew there was some pushing and shoving and Stringbean had to break them up. "Really? Come on guys, let's get it together." After some explanation James was satisfied, kinda apologized and went off in a huff. Off in the distance was James' wife, Bell. She had been petulant all morning because the cookies for her sale table had burned a bit on the edges and she wanted to sell them anyway. "Some folks like them that way," she said. James would not have it. "You have time to bake a few batches tonight. Whaddaya think?" Perhaps that's why he was so testy and took it out on Boner?

Other venders continued to arrive Sunday afternoon. Of course, they wouldn't put out other than tables and chairs today, saving their goods for early Monday. Even though there were a couple of mix-ups about vendors' places and a couple of children who wanted to jump around in the rings, (they were promptly sanctioned by committee member Sarafina) and the Orb story, there was good cooperation and it looked like everything was finally going to plan.

That night after all that could be done was done, folks stayed for a BBQ (the fire for the meats had gotten hotter and hotter all day). The pulled-pork sandwich on toasted sourdough bread looked the best, Astra thought. She also got slaw and beans, and of course, some unsweet tea, very cold. It had been a hot day and even though there was a gentle breeze, well it wasn't quite fall y'all! Most of the other food was like dinner on the ground and the meat was tended to by the best BBQer in our County, Brandon. He had won contest after contest, not only in our County but all over the state and nationally. We loved his stuff. Over forty-five folks stayed and ate! The *GentleSpirits* played a bit of music and a few committee members and others even got up and danced.

++

Labor Day morning was overcast and a wee bit rainy. No, not a big rain, or even a storm forecasted, just a tad mushy, and that caused apprehension about mud, especially in the circles. Hopefully the humidity would come down as the day advanced. Likely would dry out before the competition began. The practice ring was tested about 10:30am and by 1pm all should be ready to go!

Folks had packed up last night after the BBQ and were ready at 7am to get over to the field and set up. Vendors came from far and wide, registrations took place until 10am, and the six Referees appeared, checked out their circles and got their 'uniforms'. There were three Final Judges and they came ready to work. All had matching lime-green T-shirts that said:

DOGWOOD MARBLE JUBILEE
CHOCTAW COUNTY, MS.

on one side and then either *REFEREE* or *JUDGE* on the other. Very spiffy really, colorful and easily identifiable. Each of the players chose either a bright fluorescent pink or orange t-shirt with *MIBSTER* on the front, and received a *gen-u-wine* marble bag and rules when they checked in. The littlest kids were such a hoot to watch, their proud parents hanging on to their hands and trying to help them get their stuff. Nevaeh was no exception. At nine she was one of the older Kid mibsters and she was quite able to do all she needed to so neither Percy nor Beatrice were hovering about. Nevaeh intended to win it all.

++

Probably one of the highlights for Astra, (though there would be a couple more) was the arrival of Mark's glass-blowing RV. In order for his exhibitions to schools and groups like ours to work, he had, needless to say, repurposed the whole inside. The only thing remaining marginally original was the drivers and front seats. That's it. Everything else had been gutted and replaced by the little studio and the little shop at the far end, where he had jars of glass beads, marbles, buttons, and the like.

He and his team had made them over the last year and they were ready for purchase, some were very inexpensive, well, except for a few. He had paperweights and orbs, and even a jar of *marrididdles* a friend had made. Anyway, Mark arrived around 7am and it took him a couple of hours to get set-up. Because the Orb required his big 2,000+ degree ovens back at his studio he brought it *almost* finished so he could torch it bringing it to the finish. He had been blowing glass marbles and orbs since he was eleven so he loved sharing his work especially with the Tweens.

People were already coming in and every $2.50 raised was money for the County food banks. Some folks also brought canned goods and the barrels began to fill. There is always something sweet and simple we can do, Astra pondered. Always something.

Beatrice wandered over to the Registration table now closed about half an hour wanting to see who was in each circle. There were two in each of the two Senior Circles, two in the Adult, two in the Young Adult, in the Teen, two in the Tween, and two in the Kids. These had all reached this stage by winning their Regionals. They almost had to have another Kids circle but an eight and six year old dropped out. She noticed something that shocked her. Besides Bagger, Boner and James, Astra was competing in one of the Senior circles! Right and against James! She hadn't mentioned it to anyone so Beatrice figured she'd not comment at this time. It was nearing 11am and time for those who wanted to come and see Mark's exhibition. The three Judges, Andrew, Knock and Delta, met to confirm times, places and rules. They met with the six Referees and shared the same. It was almost time for the games to begin. The mibsters would meet with them at 3:45pm and the Championship game would begin at 4pm.

++

Finally, it was time for Mark's exhibition. Folks were gathering and despite the music blaring in the background, most could be heard one to another. There was plenty of room for all to see and hear as Mark was a bit elevated. JasonMa had the music cut off, introduced Mark who received wonderful applause and welcome, then the crowd hushed.

"I am so happy to be with y'all today for your Marble Jubilee. I hope I can share with all you marble lovers some insight on how your precious taws and kimmies were made and finish the Orb that will be part of your grand -prize." Folks whooped. "I come from a small studio called *HandBlown Glass Designs* near Tuscaloosa in Alabama. We are a team of five working together since 1997. We specialize in orbs, paperweights, and marbles, though we have designed some lamps, cups, animals and the like for special orders. We have three ovens each over 2,000degrees. That's mighty hot! I brought a UTUBE video that will make a little clearer the actual process and then I have some bits and pieces ready to finish. We'll make a marble from beginning to end. This video is of my friend Jim Mongrain a master gaffer, of the Hot Glass Demonstration Team. He works with ovens and glass at about 2,300degrees! Let's watch. He will show you some of the techniques I'll follow up with."

So the very interested folks gathered closer to the fifty-two inch screen secured to the RV wall and watched Jim and his team make a beautiful glass dragon. When it was finished Mark took out some clear and colored canes, his torch, and tools (tweezers, shears, scissors) and began to gather the hot glass onto a steel rod until it was about half the size of what would be finished. People stood awestruck as the glass grew and twisted. Then he began to add the molten colored glass stick onto the clear blob until it was twisted into a swirl. Then he repeated the process and covered it all with clear glass until it was about two inches. He rolled it on the metal- topped table to be sure it was without nicks and then fitted the toebreaker glob into the metal marble mold. Mark twisted it, rolled it and kept it warm with the torch so it would not crack, and then he brought around the scissors, cut a little nick onto the cane and tapped it. The stick broke off. He finished the marble by smoothing off the nipples and Bob's yer uncle…there was a beautiful two inch *toebreaker,* its core was a blue and green swirl. Folks were astonished. Mark put it in a very cool (but very warm) oven to finish it and keep it from cracking.

Oh my, thought Astra, time had flown by and the moment had come. Folks felt quite educated about how to make a marble, now who was going to win with their favorite marbles?

Andrew's very big, bold voice gave him the job to announce the rules for the mibster competitors and the assembly. He had a small portable mic but really didn't need it.

"The final games from the Regional contests begin now and will lead to the Championship Ring Game around 4pm. It is my pleasure to welcome y'all to our County and for all the players, Referees, and families to enjoy today. Let me introduce the six Referees and our three Final Judges." And he did. "Now let me review the rules that will apply to each circle no matter the age group. The circles and shooting lines have been adapted in each case and made age appropriate." And he did. "You may only compete in your age group and at the Ring assigned. Each one has ten marbles (except the Championship Final where you may have fifteen) in a particular color different from your opponent. Who will go first is established by whoever gets closest to the center of the kimmies 'X'. When you flick your marbles, they must be shot from the line outside the circle. When it is your turn, you will attempt to strike the opponents marble and cause it to roll outside the circle. YOU MUST KEEP YOUR KNUCKLES ON THE GROUND when you shoot, or a foul will be called and your opponent will play. There is a Referee at each circle. These are all keepsies so if you are successful you keep that marble and continue. If you miss or the marble does not go out it will be the other player's turn. And so on. The winner will be declared who has the most marbles and will move on to the Final. Do any of the players have any questions?" None were raised. These had been the rules for the last three months at every level of play. "Great then report to your Ring and let the games begin."

Andrew wiped his brow and his rather bald and shiny head with a white handkerchief (he frequently used when he preached) and sat down. Beatrice came over and they chatted. Mark was working hard in the RV finishing-up a few bits but mainly the *HandBlown Glass Orb* for the Grand Prize Winner. He didn't have long to accomplish it.

There was some music in the background but the mibsters often preferred it quiet so they could concentrate on their play. Nevaeh was well into her game, having hit the center of the kimmies. Max was waiting for his turn, still confident he could win. Sherrilynn was nervous as her opponent was a big important boy she didn't like much. Roderick was sure he was going to win the Young Adults, Jasper and Jean were playing it close for the Adults. Bagger and Boner struggled to win the Seniors. Astra and her opponent were ready to go. She used some agate marbles with an orange cat's eye shooter.

The clock ticked by and each Ring was full of anticipation and mystery, who would win, and then who would WIN the big Championship game?

The bell sounded over the mic to end the games. The Referee counted each mibster's marbles and declared their winner. Andrew called to each Referee to announce the name of their Finalist.

"Kids." ONE shouted back, "Nevaeh". Folks cheered and shouted. She smiled almost embarrassed but still poised to win big.

"Tweens." TWO barked back: "Max". He was sure he would be the big winner now. He had won over nine marbles from his opponent and lost only three. "Teens". THREE reported: "Sweeny". Again there were claps and hopes for the best. "Young Adults". FOUR announced: "Patience". "Adults". FIVE resoundingly bellowed: "Jasper" and finally "Senior Division." He tossed it over to Referee SIX. "Judges as you know there were two Senior circles and so at the end of time there was a winner in each one. Following that we had a play-off with *marrididdles* between Boner and Astra and Boner is the winner." Folks cheered as the Finalists lined up near the Judge's table. They each got a new hot yellow T-Shirt that said **MIBSTER JUBILEE FINALIST** and were whisked away for an hour of rest and refreshment.

The crowd broke up and went this way and that for cold drinks, that rainy morning thing had long gone and there was a hot sun and blue skies. A perfect day. The vendors made sure their commodities were ready for sale and the music was at the max. A good variety of R&B, Country, a little hip-hop and even some soulful Gospel filled the air while folks began to get ready for the Final. Beatrice had checked in with Mark and the Orb was finished. It was a beautiful silver and gold fumed twist, cooling for another couple of hours before the presentation. Who wouldda thought?

The hour passed quickly and the Finalists, Neveah, Max, Sweeny, Patience, Jasper, and Boner came out of the A/C tent where they had been resting. Each one looked so proud, a little nervous (even the older ones) and ready to play. Today was the day they'd practiced for at least the last three months and they each wanted to win the *Silver Cup* and the *HandBlown Glass Orb.* Why they'd even seen the way the Orb was made and were anxious to take it home with them.

Folks from the teams gathered around Astra amazed that she had participated and won one game. "When I started I never thought I could get down to the ground," she began, "really I never thought I could get back up! Then with a little practice and a few aches and pains I became more able to play." Everyone laughed as her red hat fell off and she picked it up and dusted it off. "That was the most fun I've had in years. I'd never played with *marrididdles* before. I was glad I won a few. The clay makes a nice contrast to the glass. I hated to lose some of my agates! You know my marbles are years old?" (Now she was on a roll). "Why wooden and clay marbles go all the way back to

Egypt. Those marbles made out of animal bone were considered to have spiritual meaning. Another gift from Africa! Even the Roman poet, Ovid, mentions playing marbles in his poem, *Nux*! There are reports that Caesar Augustus played marbles! In 1675, the Dutch played with stone marbles. No doubt they had been ground some way or rounded by water pressure. In the 1800s folks played with clay ones. They could never be perfectly round but that was OK. The clay was white usually and had kaolin in it. Did I tell you that the handmade glass ones in 1840, were first made in Lauscha, Germany? It took 2,000 cubic meters of timber to keep their ovens burning per year so when they ran out of wood, they had to move. Nuns and Monks were the first to run glassworks (that was before 1400!) because they could read the glass recipes in Latin! There was sand (of course, that's what glass comes from when highly heated) or volcanic limestone that was used and the glass was greenish because of the iron and it was called Waldglas (*forest glass*). So from about 1856 to 1916, handmade glass marbles, canes, colored glass balls and knobs were in demand. Am I going on and on?" Folks smiled politely and probably wanted to move on but if Astra wasn't finished they wanted to hear the rest.

"No, go on," they encouraged her. So she did but not for much longer.

"Well, the marble making machine came after WW I so marbles, called 'commies' were mass produced. These common marbles are still made today mostly in China, Mexico, and West Virginia, USA. But there are still handmade ones in small and large studios and we've witnessed one today." Folks clapped. "Now, for my last point. It concerns the World Marble Championship. There may be one this year but can anyone tell us who the Champion was in 2015? It was held in Prague." People looked about at each other and there was an ignorant silence. Astra smiled having stumped them, and said: " Lena Nedvedova. You can look that up and see how *you* might play for the USA in the next World Marble Championship. Let's go see the rest of the presentations!"

She took a breath, wandered over to a little chair, drank a bottle of cold water and refreshed she got up and ambled around. Weren't all our team members fantastic, Astra thought and noticed Whiplash looking over her way. And all the volunteers? We have had an amazing day and it's not over yet. Do we have all the prizes ready for the presentation? JasonMa was at the table and showed them all off. Folks ooooed and aahhhed and wished they were winning some of them. But no, only the winners of each circle would be presented with these incredible additions to their collections. Fortunately, most of those packs for prizes were available at one or another vendor's stand. Then he lifted up the *Silver Cup* and simply mentioned that the *Orb* was cooling and would be ready at the proper time.

Melodious and Sarafina were eating some pulled-pork sandwiches, watermelon slices (with fennel cake to follow) and drinking sweet tea while chatting with Crystal and Olive. Stringbean was close by making sure the Championship Ring was ready. He'd swept it several times and had some 'crime scene tape' around the edge to prevent others from accidently passing over. Sgt. Peason had donated it and it worked a treat.

Nevaeh was sure she was going to win and told Percy so. "I have to win. I love that Orb. You know it's six inches big or even ten. (Actually, it was four inches and glowing.) You don't play with it, or I don't think you do, you put it on a little stand. I love it and I want to win it." Percy smiled, hugged her little sis, and encouraged her just to go out and have fun and to do her best. Beatrice came by for a little group hug and Nevaeh moseyed over to the table where she was supposed to meet. Max was equally sure he was going to win. "I had the best technique," he bragged, "in the Tween section. I bet it's even better than the Seniors!" Maybe so maybe not. Anyway, he was going to try. The others remained quiet and wandered over to the Judges table as well. Bagger was a little blue that he'd lost to Boner. He was his brother after all.

The three Judges, Andrew, Knock and Delta gathered them at the table and had a moment of silence. Then Andrew reminded them about being good sports and fair competitors. He thanked them for participating and asked them to take their place around the circle. It was single elimination so Sweeney and Boner would go first. Then that winner and Nevaeh and so on. When the first half were ousted the remainder were paired off again to arrive at the Championship Winner. Stringbean had removed the yellow tape and all was ready. The music was silenced, the onlookers hushed. It was time for THE *Dogwood Marble Jubilee Championship.* The clock struck 4pm, the bell rang and play began. Each of the three pairs played for twenty minutes with fifteen marbles each. Those left standing then did the same until there was one mibster with the most marbles. Sweeny had won first start in his and off he went. After winning five marbles he failed to get another. Then it was Boner's turn. He got six and that was it. Max unfortunately shot but didn't have his knuckles down and so a foul was called. He was out only ending up with four marbles. Nevaeh won ten marbles. It went on to Boner who got twelve marbles and then Patience and Jasper were out three marbles each, so the Championship Final was Nevaeh and Boner. Who would finish as the Champion? They were ready to play. And they did. The bell rang and it was all over. Who had won???

++

The newspaper, on the day following Labor Day and the Marble Jubilee, was happy to cover all the winners and the Grand Prize Winner. A great reporter wrote an article about Bagger who won the ' *Taw shooter over fifty years old*' prize. He figured it was about 85 years old, given him on a choosing day when he was five (he's now sixty-five). Pop-Paw Bagger told him he thought it was about thirty-five years old then…you do the math. Anyway it was a great article and Bagger won a 3/4" 1950's *OLD GRAMPIE* (with dings) handmade Latticino solid core swirl with pontils (those little cuts where the cane was cut off on each end, but left to set). He was thrilled. He had nothing in his collection like it even though he said he thought he had over 500 marbles!

The Silver Cup and *HandBlown Glass Orb* (with beautiful hardwood stand) went to Boner. Already engraved was :

THE DOGWOOD MARBLE JUBILEE,
CHOCTAW COUNTY, MS.

and soon it would have Boner's name as well. As mentioned, the Orb was a gold and silver fume twist, handmade by Mark and finished right there on the grounds in his RV studio!

Runner-up was Nevaeh. Her prize was a one inch *GALACTIC VORTEX* (with stand) handmade by Fabien Jauget from Luxembourg <u>and</u> an all-expenses paid visit to Mark's *GlassDesign* studio in Tuscaloosa for a master lesson in marble- making. She was so chuffed. Beatrice and Percy were over the moon (they'd get to go too) and all the other kids cheered her because it wasn't easy playing adults. She'd lost to Boner but they hugged and there were photo ops all over the place. The other four who competed in the Championship each won a book: *MARBLE COLLECTORS HANDBOOK* by Robert Block. The newspaper was full of pics of winners and on-lookers, of committee members and teams. It had been quite a day. Oh, and the big surprise from Mark to Beatrice and ' *the dogwood*' team was a four inch Memorial Paperweight with a large colorful turquoise and gold Galactic swirl for the science center. Inside it said:

DOGWOOD MARBLE JUBILEE
CHOCTAW COUNTY
GO MIBSTERS! SHOOT YER KIMMIES.

On the very bottom was etched *GlassDesign*, Tuscaloosa, AL. and the date. The paperweight was really something special and '*the dogwood*' visitors for a very long time would happily view it and those who were in it could tell their story, bringing it alive again. There isn't much more to tell about this very big Jubilee except folks decided they would have one every two years. Have you visited York, Nebraska's Marble Museum opened in 1954? Lee Batterton has antique German and USA handmade and machine made for viewing, AND when the kids come in, they get a free bag! "Next time yer in Nebraska," Astra pointed out, "you will have a rare treat!"

Astra had begun to fade.

As folks were dispersing, Astra gathered friends and passed out more information. "Get this. Have you heard of Brian Pankey? Well, *he bounced a ½" marble on a hockey puck for 7minutes 49.13 seconds.* Who knew; either the marble collectors or the hockey players maybe and now you do too!" They all howled with laughter. She also passed on that Marcie had decided to open a little shop right there in Choctaw County selling marbles and paperweights. She and Mark had talked (and walked) and found they had a lot in common and business and well…who knows?

THE END

10

Astra Fisic and Thee Café Makeover

Unlikely as it may seem Astra Fisic and her many friends from town and County wanted to do a makeover of Thee Café. SueSue Clarion, the owner, was not so sure. It would cost lots of money she figured; there would be problems with the chairs and tables. Would business cease during the makeover? Not sure just why she'd have to lose money because her place was big enough for many guests and sections could be cordoned off, thought Astra.

Dog, Astra's bi-polar puppy who could only cope with such a name wanted to go every time she went out. But no, didn't go! Melodious says it was because the dog's temperamental and a bit wonky. Dog is one year old and has been a constant companion of Astra's since baby-puppyhood, rescued from the shelter with her bi-polar condition and despite it has proven a wonderful companion. There are several hilarious stories, however, we might hear about later (or not), making Dog the perfect target both for those who like to make fun of others and those who can use a little humor to buck up their sagging hearts. Astra hired the only dog-sitter she knew that Dog loved, Winky. She anticipated no problems. Dog had her medicine at breakfast. Winky was a hugger and Dog loved her. They both need naps and distractions to keep from unwanted depression.

++

Some time back, you might remember the building of '*Dogwood Stars Science Center*'...in the railcar (usually called '*the dogwood*')? Anyway, that might remind you of how many folks wanted their town and County to have very interesting and homemade things about for themselves and their visitors. The disused railcar was painted, repurposed and it was the neighbors who built shelves, closets, bookcases and desks. Why they even built steps and ladders, the ramp and bicycle rack outside. They liked genuine, they liked authentic, and they liked original. They liked to share. So the Thee Café makeover evolved you might say, not only because lots of townies commented upon it's need, but because folks wanted to spiffy up the neighborhood's Main Street and help SueSue. Folks also very much liked the place and SueSue and wanted the help. Thee Café and '*the dogwood*' are at opposite ends of town at the ends of Main Street. Perfect! One could go to the museum or other Dogwood activities and then head up the road to Thee Café for lunch or dinner (breakfast until 10:30am).

Astra was getting excited as she called a small meeting her best collaborators. She had asked Alcor, artist, to head up the project design who brought a very comprehensive report and wonderful drawings. Soon the little committee would be melding back into the big committee and the project would be underway. In the small group was Rockwell, science teacher at the local Community college and veteran of '*the dogwood*' project and Dr. Hanna Edana, Director of the Dogwood. Also a very important part of the small committee was SueSue Clarion, owner of Thee Café. Her husband Butch resided in a wheelchair (as did Dr. Hanna) but was quite into painting and the like. Butch was a funny guy and he kept others laughing. "The first things to be restored, repurposed, and re-gifted to the community were the tables and chairs. SueSue could tell you where each of the chairs and tables came from." Astra kept getting more excited and could see (as if in a dream) what it might look like when all was well. Thee Café had been open since the late 40's and when SueSue thought about her grandfather, MoseyJoe (they only called him that because he worked at such top speed) first opened it after WW II. He didn't talk about it much. Anyway, SueSue was a caring person and loved Thee Café. It was obviously a way to make a living (for her, her two cooks (Kisha and Jose), and store manager (Roxanne), to provide healthy and well cooked food for customers, and she liked the idea that it had become over the years a place for people to meet and plan. Unfortunately until the mid 60's, black people were not allowed to dine in. They could buy take –out at the back door connected to the kitchen, and SueSue never understood, when she was a child what was up (MoseyJoe and Clemmie just told her 'that was the way things were.'). Mexicans and 'others' weren't allowed in either. Later she made sure when she and Butch took over that nothing like that happened again! Everyone was welcome and she hired folks to work for them over the years who came from a variety of backgrounds.

MoseyJoe and his wife, Clemmie had two children, SueSue and her brother, Michael. Michael had gone off in the 60's and never returned to the South. He had always hated working in the kitchen and feeding the poor or black people from that split back door. No one was quite sure why he really left as he'd graduated HS here and even went to college. He just plain disappeared. They'd checked to see if he was kidnapped or killed. No evidence. Wasn't in jail as far as they could discover. SueSue had stayed on, took over Thee Café when her parents retired, and never looked back. Sometimes she wondered where Michael had gone. Who knew? It left her with a hole in her heart as they were only two years apart. Unfortunately, her parents never spoke of him and if his name was ever raised in conversation they would simply say he was dead. (I guess that was sorta true as he was dead to them.) MoseyJoe and Clemmie were married in 1951 and his parents gave them Thee Café for a wedding present. He'd worked there as a teenager and loved the place. It had a little back room where they could live until the house MoseyJoe had in mind was built. SueSue was born in 1953 and Michael came along in 1955.

Thee Café was much smaller then and it took a few years to build on here and there, purchase chairs, tables and equipment, and to make a go of it. In fact, MoseyJoe and Clemmie decided to collect tables and chairs from wherever they went to make the interior of Thee Café clearly original. And so they did. Now things were beginning to wear and needed some restoration. Would the locals want to get into such a project? Who knows? Anyway Astra would ask. SueSue felt Astra was quite confident that this would be the 'funnnnest' project ever!

++

Astra Fisic, that slightly retired astronomer who always wears a red hat, had begun to doodle in an old sketchbook. Alcor had left it behind after the painting was finished on the railcar and so it was a bit of a trip down memory lane for Astra. Here were all Alcor's sketches of the summer sky and it's triangle of Vega, Deneb and Altair. Now they shone on the side of 'the dogwood' all year long. The other sketches included various stars, practiced lettering, and of course, Jupiter's four prominent moons (she has sixty-nine!) and Saturn with her rings ringing. Oh my, Astra thought, I have got to get going myself. This is such a beautiful book I think I'll switch to an old ring binder I have and do my sketches on plain paper. She carefully put the sketchbook away, a treasure she'd one day return to Alcor. Astra began doodling turning basic to creative chairs that one would find in Thee Café; they would become magic works of art. She wasn't sure there needed to be much to be done on the thirty-two booths…maybe just on the strip of wood along the top

125

and the metal pole that held up each booth table. Astra tried drawing a long strip and using her best markers affixed a design. She was not an artist she just had good ideas, as Alcorn would tell her. Alcor will be able to turn these into sketches, plans, and eventually we would get the makeover made over! She was delighted as she sat hugging Dog and rocking in her favorite chair. One minute she was grumpy (like the sisters) and the next as sweet as she could be. One minute she wanted to play and the next she wanted a good fight. She would nip Astra's ankles and then look up with pleading eyes for a treat. Astra loved that Dog and she cherished their time together. Alcor bounced into Astra's place with a new sketchbook. She wanted to share some of what she'd been doing and see if it was along the lines they envisioned. They spent the afternoon talking about chairs, tables, booths, and floors, and well everything in the end.

"I was trying to figger out how many chairs there really are," Alcor said. "Do you know?"

Astra shook her head but having booted up her computer she turned to the calculator and multiplied 25 tables x 4 equaling 100 and then there were the 8 tables with 2 chairs each, that's 16, and finally there were those tables with only one chair hidden off in the corner. That would be 12. Final score: 128 chairs. Oh there are 45 tables and 32 booths (all 4 seaters).

"Good Lord, that's a lot," squeaked Alcor, "really a lot. We can't do that in a weekend!"

"No but I have an idea. SueSue knows where each chair came from and you will be amazed to know some come from out of the country, like Mexico or Japan. So if we can get a basic design for each chair then each person who wants to donate can take the chair home and paint it. We'd charge a basic fee to get a chair, say $20; then paint, design and necessaries would be provided by SueSue. I would take a chair home. It would have a sombrero and certain color schemes that show a Mexican flavor for the new design. When I return it and the necessaries, I will be able to put my name on it. When all are finished (those that are wooden) we will varnish and seal them at the same time. Would reduce the smelly! The ones with aluminum can be shined up and the seats painted or material refurbished. Whaddya think?"

Alcor's eyes lit up. "You amaze me. When do you dream this stuff up?"

"Well, this one I thought about during the *Dogwood Marble Jubilee*. Actually, I had considered it about a year ago, and when I tried it out on SueSue she wasn't very accepting. Hadn't answered enough questions or shared the vision enough. Even so I think she was very interested because about six months ago she asked me if I had any drawings of what a make-over might look like."

"We also have to consider the booths. There are thirty-two and each one has a wooden strip across the top. I don't think we need to do much more than clean the seats and their tables. If the strip and the pole holding the table up are painted some bright colors seems that would help a lot? Some look dingy if not close to rusted."

"We also have to consider the floor, the shopping area, and the kitchen. Her equipment isn't all the way top of the line but SueSue replaced an oven a couple of years ago and a freezer before that. We could get one of the team to assess what they think she really needs, maybe only a good clean at this stage? The serving-line needs a general uplift. SueSue said she was already considering a change round for the shopping area so we'd just let her get on with it." Astra looked tired. Alcor went into her kitchen and made them a pot of mint tea. They rested a bit.

"Oh," said Alcor. "We will need to consider the windows and the sign. These won't take long to paint or design once we think it up! We may need a new front window. It will make a big first impression and that is important for business. It will also set the stage for what folks will see when they come in to dine! You know the original name of Thee Café is: *Uptown Downtown Only One In Town MAIN STREET CAFÉ* ? It will be fun to try to work that into some part of the decoration. What about the walls?"

Astra was nodding a bit. "I think I need a nap," she yawned. "Perhaps we can consider that next time?" Alcor agreed, packed up her stuff, kissed Astra on the cheek, let Dog in and set off home. Dog and Astra headed for her bed and snoozed for a good two hours. When she awoke, Dog was 'smiling' in her face, licking her kisses.

++

Raymond was new to town. Well, he had only been back about ten years and you know how that goes, even twenty hardly means you can say 'yer from here'! Anyway, he attended Church with Beatrice, Nevaeh and Percy and was a wall painter, a house painter. One Sunday after services they were chatting over coffee and Beatrice asked him if he'd be interested in Thee Café project. Raymond wanted more information and Beatrice discovered he'd not been at Thee Café very often. He told her he occasionally got gas there or jumped into the store part and bought some food. Otherwise, he wasn't a regular like the rest of them.

"Well," Beatrice began, "that's quite alright. Some of the folks in town are discussing possibly giving Thee Café a makeover and we will need someone who understands painting walls and the outside of the building. Do you think you might be interested?"

Raymond was a shy guy, a bachelor, thirty-eight years old. He had moved back to the County to take care of his aging parents. Within that time they both passed and so he worked his job, owned the company his daddy left him, and well, read a lot and collected stamps. He was a weekly churchgoer but that was about all and he didn't like meetings much but supported his local NAACP. Raymond was lean and strong, wore white paint pants (covered in a variety of colors) and a red t-shirt with their company's logo on the front: a very large gold paintbrush with bold black writing: **PaintWRITE** . Why, they could paint your house or do the lettering for your business. Just ask. They were the best in the County! He had a very long open wooden tool- box with brushes, scrapers, rags and other equipment he might need. Raymond's younger sister, Dilette, was still in grad-school at Vanderbilt in Nashville studying medicine. She was unmarried and twenty-eight and soon she would be a medical doctor concerned for the little ones, a pediatrician. He was very proud of her and helped her financially when he could. They were the only family they had left so they got together as often as possible. Raymond particularly loved driving up the Natchez Trace to Nashville. Seemed no matter what time of year there was something beautiful to see. The speed limit was very slow (fifty mph) so one could take in all its glory. He had just returned from a visit when he and Beatrice began their conversation.

"Yea, I went to visit my sister," he told her, "she is a medical student at Vanderbilt and wants to take are of vulnerable kids, preemies, those in the Nic-U. I would cry all the time, I think! The Trace this time of year is very beautiful."

Beatrice was touched by this big man and his soft center. His deep brown eyes sparkled behind rimless glasses and his head was a bit wooly when he took off his company cap. Was lovely to meet a young man so connected to his feelings, she thought. "Well, anyway, whaddya think about being part of our project?"

"I'll think about it and if I don't decide to help out my business partner RodX just might. Our company could certainly donate some paint, or sponsor a chair or give money or…whatever."

Beatrice smiled. "We could use you both!" She left him her number and email and set off for Thee Café for *red-white-and-blue plate* lunch (today was baked chicken, squash, and those little fried potatoes with onions and peach cobbler).

Melodious, Whiplash and Sarahfina, had gone to Thee Café for breakfast (well, a late brunch) and were still there when Beatrice and Astra came in. Alcor would come a bit later. SueSue, the owner, came over and sat with them. "I hear you are beginning to get folks together who want to participate in the makeover?"

"Yes," Whiplash suspended her eating to answer, "Yes, I think we'll have enough to make this an even more magnificent place!" She flicked her right hand up and made a funny giggling noise. She had a large (well, *very* large) summer straw hat on and when she flicked it went flying. The headband of ribbons caught on the edge of the chair at the next table and the very nice people, not expecting flying things to arrive while eating, gently passed it back to her. She went several shades of red but thanked them.

"I have a few concerns and a few ideas. Is this a good time to share them?" SueSue seemed worried.

"SueSue, this is your place and we only want to do what you want. Now we may have lots of ideas but if they're not a fit for you and your business…well…" Astra commented.

So, for the next hour or so SueSue led the conversation about the makeover with the women and when Alcor arrived with her sketchbook they got down to work. She was able to take their ideas and put them page by page into the book and as they took shape Astra, Beatrice, the sisters and SueSue were amazed at what they saw. What an artist.

"We essentially have three big rooms, a kitchen area with serving line, and the store. Each of the big rooms are different sizes but outfitted the same. You've figured out how many chairs and tables there are and how many booths. I like the idea about just cleaning up the booths and maybe adding a little painted design on this strip and the metal pole holding up the table." SueSue seemed more relaxed. "I think you know that each chair, well except for a recent few we bought on-line, are all part of our 'collection'? Over the years we brought back a chair from here or there and made it part of our 'dine-in rooms'. MoseyJoe and Clemmie had started that tradition so we kept it going when we took over. That's lots of chairs ago. Some would never have stood restoration so we chucked them out. The ones we have here are the sturdiest and will take a good paintjob and design."

"I love that, so whimsical." Alcor chimed in. "So unique and so artsy!" She could not wait to get going.

"One of the things I'm worried about is losing business while this make-over is happening. What have you thought about to keep that from happening?"

Melodious piped up, "Well, if we can get the folks in one section to take their chairs home and paint them there you can use the rest of the rooms and so on until all the chairs are done. We thought we'd just do nicely designed Formica tops for the tables and do them all at once some evening after yer closed. Any good? We'll have a lock-down (or whatever it's called) like when we were teens. Our church had one every now and then and once in, no getting out until the next morning. We slept, did activities…well, you know…so we could eat and work. " She could have gone on but realized most had moved on already.

SueSue was pleased. "I wonder if it would be worth it to just close the Café, do the chairs, and keep the kitchen and store open for take-out only?"

Sarahfina popped up and suggested that, "We could all buy our lunches and dinners here over the days we're working. That would be quite a few, maybe not as many as you'd get on a regular day but…?"

Folks looked at each other. Whiplash mentioned Raymond and RodX and thought talking to them about doing the walls first might be an idea. "We also need to talk about what you want for the floor." SueSue agreed. "If the rest of the place is going to be colorful and bold then I think the tiles need to be also." Melodious knew just the woman, a carpet and tile dealer in the next town over. She'd go visit and have her come back and give an estimate.

++

Raymond was particularly interested in his stamps. You might think that a twee thing for a grown man when he could be out doing lots of other things more rough and tumble, but it was his hobby and well, most folks need one! His uncle Roy had started him on the collecting road when he was about six and he'd never looked back. For a few years he was very careful to use the stamp books Roy brought him for Christmas or a birthday. Then as he got older he became interested in two or three specific times like 1935-1945, and then another year he only collected sports stamps, and then he was into animals and ecology. He had some stamps from round the world but he particularly collected the UK and the USA. Over the past year or so Raymond found himself marveling at the sheer art work of the stamp, no matter the date or amount. He had created his own little stamp books for his specific interests and had stopped using the big book. It was a treat to look it over now and then and to remember what he was doing as a younger person when he found or had sent to him or even purchased this or that stamp. He found it very relaxing and he could listen to his music while looking carefully at each one. What a country puts on its stamps is an art and an invitation to know about them. So, for example, we want people to know about USA birds...so we do a series. When his uncle Roy passed, he left him all his stamps and that made for some interesting finds.

++

RodX was a jovial fellow, he was as short as Raymond was tall and they made quite a pair. RodX was married to Jennile and they had one little girl named Harriet. He and Raymond had been in Vocational College together many years ago, had done their apprenticeships, earned their licenses together on a building site and decided to have a go at their own business. Raymond was just a good painter, and artist really, and RodX was the business-brain and very good at human relations. Of course he could paint, scrape and do all the things one does when painting a house. He preferred, however, to talk to the customers. RodX had long blond hair he drew back into a ponytail and stuffed up under the company cap. Sometimes at the end of the day, his face would be covered with blue or green or whatever color the house was becoming. (Even a 'clean' pair of painting whites were dazzling with design!) Took him a while to clean up but could not wait to get home to Jennile and Harriet.

The old (1925) MacGregor place was the current worksite for **PaintWRITE.** Raymond and RodX were anxious to get started. The owners grandparents had left long ago, and Larry and Louise wanted to restore it as much as possible so they could sell it and hopefully turn a good profit. It was going to cost a bundle but Larry was certain it was a good investment. The place needed cleaning out...closets and drawers, the kitchen and den were full of grandparents-stuff. They had just packed up a few things one day in 1985, and left hoping to return from their around the world trip, but stopping in Fiji they decided to stay. They also died and were buried there. The house began to deteriorate because Louise and Larry didn't have the money to keep it up. As Larry's father had died the house came to him.

"Listen," he told the painters, "anything you find you want just show me but I'm sure you can have it. The rest you can sell or take to an antique place or whatever. That might take a little off our bill?" RodX stepped in, "Done. We'll calculate as we go but I will give you a fair estimate in a couple of days." Larry and Louise were satisfied with that.

++

Alcor brought her sketchbook over to Beatrice and Nevaeh's. Percy was at work and the sisters had gone shopping. SueSue was coming by for lunch and they felt the conversation had moved along enough to begin to design an advertising leaflet. They wanted to put it out all over the town (and County) so that folks would 'adopt' a chair, donate $20, pick it up, paint it, bring it back, put their name on it, and contribute to the most unusual Café anywhere (especially Mississippi.).

Nevaeh had produced the lunch: Avocado on 9-grain toasted bread with a little mayo (and tomato if wanted), a few baked chips, and some mac and cheese. For dessert, she had made her first peach cobbler (with a little help from Beatrice). A spot of vanilla ice cream or cool-whip was available. For drinks she offered fizzies, non-fizzies, or water. Whadda lunch! She was very happy to serve her guests (having also set the table) and all ate while complimenting her. SueSue said she'd hire her in a minute for the Café kitchen! She also cleared the table and did the dishes when it was all finished. Alcor said she could sit in on the meeting and that they'd do dishes together later. Nevaeh was pleased. She loved Alcor and always secretly wanted to be just like her, an artist.

Astra began. "We're up to 100 people who want to take and paint a chair. We might need another thirty or so. The leaflet is everywhere so we are expecting more calls. I checked with RodX who seemed to know everyone and he's lined up some carpenters who will do the Formica tops for the tables and any other wood sorts of things we might need. Some of that labor was donated; SueSue was so grateful.

"Raymond is a great stamp collector and you might wonder what that has to do with this? Well look at this wall in the biggest room." She turned it over to Alcor who showed them the suggested design. "Raymond brought me this Mississippi stamp, the guitarist with the date 1817. That was the year MS became a state and so in 2017 it became a stamp! He wants to paint that on the biggest wall!" Folks clapped and drew breath because Alcor's drawing was so beautiful and Raymond's idea so exciting. She'd used watercolors on the good watercolor paper providing a lovely texture.

"He will make an exact replica of the stamp and then set it in some color palate that will pop! He wasn't quite sure yet but agreed to meet with me in a couple of days to try out this or that. I think it will be magic. The stamp is so strong with its reds and browns so a soothing lighter background might just be the thing!"

Astra continued: "We need to figure out a sort of schedule so that SueSue loses the least amount of business. When it's all finished we'll have a grand re-opening and that will bring lotsa folks." Agreement all around and SueSue took charge of the calendar and decided that, "the project would formally begin after Easter. Let's see that's April 16 this year and hopefully be done by Mother's Day in May. Maybe the grand re-opening could be around then, free lunch for all moms etc.? I'm not sure it will take that long but I'm going to block out all that time. Here's what I've got: 1)scrub down, 2) do walls, 3)do floors, 4) do Formica tops, and 5)do booths. Obviously, the chairs are being done in people's homes and we will set a date for them all to come here. I will at the same time be scrubbing and renewing the kitchen and the store. We will have take-out and we can still sell gasoline. Whaddya think?" Sarahfina spoke for the rest… "FABULOUS indeed FABULOUS! Let's gitter done."

++

The old MacGregor place had begun to look very different. Raymond and RodX had brought on a few skilled workers to help clean out the inside. They'd found lots of things that Larry and Louise gladly let them keep and they sold other things that took money off their tab. Raymond was sure, though, that the sealed closet full of stamps, stamp books, and stamp collecting stuff, was the richest find he'd ever made when restoring a property. Louise and Larry had no feelings one way or the other and were happy to hear that Raymond was so keen. The fact that the locked closet, with a triangular door under some stairs was sealed made Raymond think there might be something very special within. He took the very best green garbage bags, bagged everything and went home. It would take him months if not years to discover what was there, even if he worked each day. There were hundreds if not thousands of stamps from all over the world and a special collection of USA Civil War stamps.

++

Stringbean (of the *Marble Jubilee* story) was in charge of paint. He was at *PerkinsPaint Store* off Main Street on Pine looking for all the colors and sizes of tins Astra and committee had ordered, some would happily be donated and the rest put on a ticket to be paid off as the $20's came in. Young Peter, son of Patrick Perkins the owner, was working that afternoon. He was nearly seventeen, getting ready to graduate from High School and go on to college. He had hoped to go to the Coast Guard Academy but no luck. So he decided to head for the Merchant Marine Academy. He would begin next August. He loved the water he loved the sea. That gave Peter plenty of time to help with the project. His dad was happy to participate and though he needed to make a living, he could donate and give a bit off here and there for the Café. Patrick ate at Thee Café frequently so it was a sort of win-win. Peter went out back and began to gather up some extra painting things his dad had set aside and loaded them in the company pickup, driving it around to the front. Stringbean and he loaded the rest onto the beds of both pickups and headed over to Thee Café.

"How about some lunch?" Stringbean offered. "On Me!"

"Why not?" Peter shot back, "I'm hungry all the time!" He was still a growing boy nearing 6' but hoping for 6'2" or so. And could he eat.

++

Well, it was time and SueSue and the team were ready to begin the big makeover of Thee Café. Over 120 people had come and taken a chair (or two) home along with the suggested design, paint and brushes. The return date was May 13 at the latest and May 1 at the earliest. May 20, a Sunday that year, was Mothers' Day. That would be the day of great celebration. They thought it funny but used April 15 (tax day) as the kick-off. A couple of the preachers from their County Association came by, gathered the team and workers asking God to bless them, especially keeping them safe as they worked.

And then with donated paint, and bought paint, scrubbing brushes, cleaning materials, scrapers, rags and newspapers the first group got underway. Demolition Day they called it and the fifteen or so volunteers scrambled to their places, aprons, paint-pants, and other assorted 'old clothes' in view. Raymond and RodX did take some time off from the MacGregor place to come and paint the walls. Louise and Larry brought home two chairs and were willing to do a few more. Raymond found stamps of *Elmo and Zoe* from Sesame Street's 50th anniversary set. Those would brighten the walls of another section a corner of the smallest room would be re-designed for kids (and a grannie). Raymond was overjoyed! Three stamps! A donated recliner would sit in the corner with a little area rug for grannie or new mom to relax.

RodX was painting the kitchen walls (a cheerful yellow), the walls around the store (a beautiful sea green). Raymond and he painted the other walls. They were still working on the exterior design and trying to decide about the windows, especially the big front one. Raymond had done some designs for the lettering and he and Alcor were still not finished. The discussion was underway about whether to use the 'original' name or *Thee Café*. Alcor and Raymond drew several options in the sketchbook and took them to RodX, the lettering man. One thing that was agreed was the exterior face of the Café would be a bright mural depicting some of the highlights of the County. This would include the Choctaw Nation, early settlers, African-Americans, Hispanics and the Scots-Irish all doing things for the County. They wanted it to go right up to the building of the new Hospital and the new addition to the High School.

Day by day the project took on color and form and SueSue seemed so happy. Not only was the place cleaned up (well it was a mess under construction but cleaner) it was a wonderful place to greet, meet, and eat. Final decisions about windows and walls were agreed, and put in the sketchbook. Alcor was in the shop trying to figger out how to best paint around all the stuff. Raymond had finished all the open walls and she saw no need to move all the goodies...but the walls were dirty. The little restrooms were freshened up, new toilet seats and urinals, hand sanitizers and a little art work on the walls. It is amazing really what a coat of paint can do to a recently dreary and yukky looking bathroom. The place was well, the same, but different. Everywhere in Thee Café was getting a new face-lift. Soon the smell of paint would be history and only the aroma of the very good food would prevail.

The three sisters were in charge of calling those who had taken a chair to see if they were going to make the deadline. Some yes, some no. The no's were offered a helper. That seemed to go well with folks who thought it would be so easy and found that furniture painting, well any painting, was a little energy intense. So far it looked as if all the 128 chairs would be done by May 13. Easter was just around the corner. The new floor was in by Easter so everyone decided to take a few days off to celebrate. They would be back at it on April 18. Next would be all the Formica tops, and cleaning up the booths and adding their new bits of design. The kitchen was clean as a whistle, and there was even a new stove/oven (in addition to the older one) and two new sinks. The floors popped with bright squares painted like a checker- board and there were several more safety strips, especially near the sinks, so whoever was working there might not slip. The fridge and freezers had been cleared out and stuff moved around. Of course, they were still cooking take-out so it wasn't completely shut down, except those days before Easter. Now there was about a month to go. All the big things were nearing completion but the little details needed attention.

++

Gregory Smalls, who worked over at the Animal Shelter, had taken a couple of chairs home and was working out in his garage, just finishing one. The seats popped out and he chose hot glue would be best and maybe use his nail gun in a couple of spots. The seat was covered with a vinyl sort of material (50's best). They weren't that cheap plastic of the 70's so he just cleaned them up and did his painting. Now he was ready to finish the second one. Gregory pushed the seat out, laid it on the workbench and began painting the chair frame. His phone rang and he had to go. Later on, he thought, I'll get it done. He hurried over to the shelter to discover a litter of puppies just born but rejected. There were six and they had not yet opened their eyes. Really cute, he thought, but we don't really have room for six puppies. What to do?

Gregory ended up bringing them home and being such a good VetTech he knew what to do. A large alarm clock wrapped in a blanket in the center of the puppy-box and it was just like mom's heart. They had to be bottle -fed and until Monday as there would be no one in the shelter. The puppies all squirmed and squiggled until they were one big ball of puppy-fur, all sleeping nicely. He took the box out into the garage, sat it down under the workbench and decided to continue with his chair. The chair frame was bright cherry red with a licorice black and bright white border all around (like a racing car flag). Was a bit tedious but he'd nothing else to do, except become a puppy-uncle. Gregory finished the frame, set it aside and decided to finish the seat as well, turning it over and saw the were some tears and the vinyl wasn't very well fastened, in fact as he moved it around the back piece fell off. To his surprise, there was a plastic sheet cover, like ones you put in your binder, taped to the seat's wood. He proceeded carefully as this was an older chair and he certainly did not want to rip or split the plastic cover. Gregory found a flat round-nosed knife and gently slid it under the plastic carefully lifting it off the seat; the tape had aged so it came off easily. Gregory sat down on his tall three-legged stool and slipped his hand into the plastic envelope. Within there was an envelope and two smaller plastic packets. He edged them cautiously out and placed them on the workbench under his halogen lamp and peered into the plastic packets. They each had a stamp, one affixed to an odd- looking envelope and the other just a stamp by itself, carefully prepared in a proper stamp-collectors cellophane covering. Perhaps there was information in the covered envelope?

Squeeakking and a little bit of crying, and one guy crawling all over the others came from the puppy-box. He let them get on with it.

On the outside of the envelope it simply said TO YOU WHO FOUND THIS.LUCKY YOU. Gregory opened it and there was a short note: *If you know nothing about stamps, especially about the very FIRST stamp (minted in UK about 1840) then here's the information. Packet ONE has a tiny envelope, contrary to regulations, with a PENNY BLACK Stamp (IL), with 4 margins. Probably worth around 300 pounds (no idea how many $$ that will be to you. May be worth a whole lot more if you don't find this for another 50years!). The second packet has an 1840 1d Penny Black Pl BG, very fine, used, Red Maltese Cross cancellation. Probably worth about 100 pounds (or more).* There was no signature only a date of 1979 and the comment: I am in prison for a very long time. Enjoy.

Gregory sat quite still and knew he needed to phone Raymond.

++

We are nearing the end of the make-over of the Thee Café. Most things you already know. Mother's Day is in about a week with the targeted RE-opening. The menu has been worked out and all the chairs and tables and everything else almost in place. The last thing to finish is the front window. The mural around is completed and they finally removed that horrible rubber rug that makes folks trip as they come in the (new) doors. The path is painted a welcoming sage blue with three long and sturdy safety strips. The glass fitters are coming to help on Tuesday. RodX's lettering is calligraphically cool and in strong black letters, large enough to see from the other end of town. He and Alcor designed it and here's what it looks like: all around the edges of the window are the words *UPTOWN DOWNTOWN ONLY ONE IN TOWN Main Street Café Established 1947* surrounded by strawberries and blueberries, sweet potatoes, greens, okra and watermelon. In the center with some very inventive contemporary painting of burgers, fish, mac 'n cheese, and *red-white-and-blue* plates is the name, right in the very center in very big letters THEE CAFÉ and under that GREET, MEET AND EAT! Y'ALL COME ON IN. MISSISSIPPI'S FINEST. Opening times and days were also very visible. Whimsical, charming, rugged, and very user-friendly Thee Café would remain one of Astra and her friend's most fun, most artistic, and most effective projects. *'the dogwood'* folks might disagree. Go figger, over 150 County and town people (that included kids of varying ages) participated one way or another and SueSue didn't lose any money during the make-over. Who knew? On the two new glass doors are SueSue and Butch's names and ancestors going back to MoseyJoe and Clemmie.

Oh, you might want to know what Raymond shouted when he found out about those two *Penny Blacks*. WOW! REALLY?WOW!OH MY GOSH!REALLY?" and so forth. For a collector who rarely had much to say, well...he was stunned and they took them onto Ebay and searched around to find a current price. Why in 2020 the one on the envelope was worth 495 pounds (or that's what it was selling for) and the other was selling for 149.99 pounds. Gregory agreed to keep the money and give the stamps to Raymond. Deal. Deal.

Gregory wanted you to know the six puppies (Australian Red Heelers) are doing well and ready to move into forever families. If you want one, phone him. They are really cute.

If yer ever in the County, do drop in and set back a spell with us. The food is great, Kisha and Jose have that worked out, the folks are mostly nice and kind and the surround is well, fabulous. Bless yer little hearts! Come on down! Astra'd love to meet ya.

THE END

11

Astra Fisic and the Underground Railroad

Here's a bit of what happened before and after the Autumn Harvest Feastival Sweet Potato Casserole Contest...

You might know Astra from her many other adventures and of course, her friends the three grumpy sisters, Melodious, Sarahfina and Whiplash. They had been friends for many years and they had grown on each other. When you share some of your life with friends over many years, you get to know them pretty well, even if you do not have as much face-time as you'd like. You might know yourself a bit better as well through their love of you.

One day over at Thee Café, during a lunch session with a *red-white-and-blue plate* (hamburger steak with brown gravy, rice, pinto beans and either a little side salad or peach cobbler and of course non/ sweet tea) Astra met up with the sisters. You know they used to be very grumpy indeed; why they are less grumpy now? Love. Plain and simple. Friendship. Mattering to someone else and learning not to be selfish. You know giving back and helping others and well, not just thinking of yourself all the time. Other people matter and even if you have to go against what might be best only for *you* so that best is for everybody, well bless yer little heart for being so brave! The sisters had learned a lot about this and so had Astra. They always said she taught them but she knew how much she had to grow and valued their friendship; what she learned from them.

"My hamburger steak is cold and tastes like shoe leather," they heard a gruff loud voice from the booth across the way. "The gravy tastes like a mud puddle. If you think that's peach cobbler, well, I do not believe it…it's like peachy cud some cow ought to be chewin'!

I'll never eat in this place again." The voice got louder and louder. A rather tall man with overalls and an old T-shirt that had clearly seen other days, but not *better* ones, arose. He doffed his old ball cap and shuffled out of Thee Café. Whiplash was astounded because she thought she was the only one who did not like the hamburger steak that day. She peered out the window and watched him try to get into an ancient- paint- scratched and rusted Ranger pickup, bumping his head, his hat falling off, almost retrieving it and then falling right down on his bottom, attempting to catch hold of the driver's seat to no avail. He plopped and just as he fell, a SUV pulled in and almost ran him over. The driver, thankfully, pulled away and got out. He was able to help him up and into the cab.

"Well, Burger, whassup?" the SUV driver asked. "Are you alright? Need to go to the doctor? What?"

"Naw, fine. ain't hurt. Just mad. Go on. But don' eat the burgersteak today. Stinky poo." Moreover, he drove off lickity-split almost crashing into a bright green VW beetle as he shot out of the parking lot.

"Well, I never," Melodious grumbled as she squeezed out of the booth. "Think of how bad the publicity is if a guy like that shouts out bad about the food?"

"Well, it ain't very good, I'm tellin' ya," Whiplash spoke in a hushed stage voice. "I'm not sure what happened, but today for the very first time in all these years I have to say, it ain't no good." She was going back to tell Jose and Kisha and give them a piece of her mind when she remembered they weren't there that day. There was a substitute cook, Darnel, who looked like a bright red boiled beet, and a woman named Lucy who stood by the stove wondering what to do next. That must be the problem. Astra had a cheeseburger, fries (no salt) and peach cobbler. She agreed it was not the best peach cobbler, but it wasn't horrid. She remembered that Burger fella from awhile back; his wife had died (Covid 19) and he was very lonesome. They got him to go to a senior program at the day care wellness center near the hospital. Then Burger got really crabby. He would throw food, spit at medical personnel, and bad mouth whomever he felt like. One day at the center Burger dove into the swimming pool and acted as if he'd never come up, swimming almost the full length underwater, just to annoy the minders. He just was so disruptive they had to ask him to leave. His son who lived in South Dakota came out and said he could move with him. Burger refused. Ernie did not know what to do so he left his dad servin' himself. Every now and then he shows up somewhere in town and has a hard time. What to do with a fella like that? He'll end up getting arrested after hurting someone, if not himself. That old pickup mostly works but looks as if it is strung together with paperclips and rubber bands; even duct tape would have helped. When Burger puts his foot on the gas, the little Ranger jumps a few feet and coughs but he often puts his foot on the gas rather than the brake and who knows who he might run into? This is dangerous for all! The local police know his patterns and suspect he acts as if laws only apply to others. They are understanding, of course, but every now and then they stop Burger, face him with some sort of ticket, hoping to remind him of the law. He sorta smiles and then hits the gas, Ranger jumps a few feet and coughs like it had bronchitis, spewing out some black smoke, swearing he will get rid of it (one day). Then he laughs out-loud. What to do? The police just quizzically look at one another, shrug their shoulders, hoping Burger will never hurt himself or others.

++

The Autumn Feastival was on the way featuring sweet potatoes and all things made from them. There would be sweet potato candy, ice cream, cakes, donuts, pies, casseroles, cookies, soup and all sorts of stuff you can hardly imagine. Astra was looking forward to it for another reason. This year she needed a vacation and the first prize was an all-expense paid trip north to Alton (and Godfrey), ILL. from Jackson, MS. on the train for a special tour of the Underground Railway sites. Astra thought it very linked that she, like slaves before her, would travel there by train. What did she have to do to win? Astra needed the very best sweet potato casserole she (or anyone else in the contest) had ever made. The Feastival lasted for three days and the judging to get to the Final 4 would be on Friday night. Folks would bring an already baked casserole for tasting by the judges; only four would remain. They would cook on site at the farm Saturday and those judges would then eliminate two, and the other two would be in the Championship Final on Sunday afternoon (so folks could go to Church).

Three judging teams one for each level. Unbelievably, the three grumpy sisters were chosen to do the Finals! They were over the moon, never imagining anyone would choose them for anything. Whiplash, Melodious and Sarahfina would get judges T-shirts, a new notepad and pen. They would be the ones to pick the Winner. Were they thrilled? You bet. Astra had to find or make-up a recipe that would wow them. 'Blind' judging would be used all three times...no names were near their entry. The judges had to judge based on presentation, texture, and yumminess. Since most of the judges were friends, Astra decided not to discuss the Feastival at all. That way no complaining, just in case she won! Rockwell, Mark (the *marble* man) and ChaChalita, from the quilt club were judging the Final 4. The Feastival was only a week away and Astra had to git cookin'.

++

It was in the midst of all this that Burger came into Thee Café. Folks who had been there the previous week sorta ducked down into their booth or hid behind their menus. He shuffled and kicked as he walked with his cane, perhaps his bottom still hurt? Burger went to the back after lookin' around and ordered a *red-white-and-blue plate* from Kisha. Jose was cooking and today it was baked chicken, black beans and greens, mac 'n cheese, cornbread and sweet tea. He headed off for the men's room and didn't come out. Not that anyone really wanted to know about his bowels or bladder, but they were concerned when Kisha came looking for him with his food.

"Bur--ger," she casually called out in a singsong lilt. "Burger, where are you sit--ting? Your food will get cold and then you'll blame me!"

"I'm sittin' on the pot. Leave me alone!" he shouted. Folks laughed and snickered a bit but were still concerned. Kisha took his food to the booth he frequented when not occupied by 'those people only interested in making him unhappy by sitting in his place.' Kisha went back to the kitchen. Marvin, one of our finest local policepersons was just finishing his lunch. Thought he would use the men's and see what was up. They both came out. Nothing said. Marvin winked at Whiplash and left. Burger sat down. Ate. Left.

Astra went home trying to brain a casserole recipe. She *googled* around, looked in her own cookbooks, especially *SOUTHERN SPECIALS* she loved dearly. Maybe I can create something out of two or three recipes, she mulled over. I know my fav is with toasted coconut, but I also love the eggnog one. Perhaps I'll discover a way to combine them? She tinkered about in her kitchen for a couple of hours trying this and that until Astra reached the taste and texture she wanted. Yup, that's it, she thought. Tomorrow I will bake for the first judges, hoping I'll make the Final 4! I really want to win that trip she thought, really want to win. For some reason I need to go to that place. Astra cleaned up the kitchen, ate the rest of the sweet potato casserole she'd made, with just a touch of cool whip, closed out the lights and sauntered off to bed. Dog was already asleep and he just rolled over, groaned a bit, gave her room to get in, and they snoozed off.

++

Whiplash, Melodious, and Sarahfina showed up right on schedule the next day for lunch at Thee Café. Also meeting them were Mark and his wife Marcie. Remember how they met during the *Dogwood Marble Jubilee* and she opened the little shop? And… Well that was a couple of years ago and now they're married and have a little peewee marble of their own, Hank. He is the cutest thing going. Mark, along with the sisters and Rockwell had come over to meet with the Feastival coordinators about being the judges for the Final 4, and Final. They all agreed a good lunch at Thee Café would be a good start. The Friday night judges were not present.

Laughing ensued when tiny Hank, about six months old, began to giggle, like outta nowhere. He saw something, heard something, felt something (perhaps gas) that tickled him and Hank laughed right out loud. Both parents, of course, beamed at the skill of their tiny child. They ate and wandered over to '*the dogwood*' for the meeting. It would only last an hour or so, rules explained especially about the tasting. Then Mark and Marcie (and Hank, of course) headed out to Tuscaloosa to home and shop, *BlownGlass Designs*. Mark had made part of the winning prize, the blown glass Orb, for the Marble Jubilee. It was striking.

This Feastival was only a week away and they all agreed to meet on the Saturday morning at Thee Café before going over to judge.

The Feastival was out at the old Parker Place this year, mostly in his repurposed barn. Lotsa folks could fit and if just by some silly quirk it might rain, well, the vendors and cooks would not be impaired. The dance Sunday night would honor the finalists and would feature square, round, and hip-hop dancing.

++

Far to the north in Alton, ILL, at *SPINACH SPECIALTIES & HEALTHFOOD STORE, MRS. DELPHI SPINACH, Owner* and *Proprietor* was at work. She'd helped design the special *NEW* tours of the Underground Railroad sites with BrandyLee her business partner and wanted her store to notch up to another level. This tour would bring hundreds of folks, thank God, that horrid virus was greatly diminished she thought. People can come out and even if they wear a mask, they will be out visiting and shopping. Delphi's shop was picturesque indeed, shelves and shelves, slightly askew from one another full of the most interesting remedies, herbs, potions, and even delicious healthy groceries. There was memorabilia about the UR as well as other interesting sites in her county and for these she had ordered T-shirts and aprons, doesn't everyone need one? There were keychains, pens, hats, the usual. She hoped to raise interest so others would come. Her favorite new item was a large poster of Alton from space indicating some of the spots where slaves might have first arrived. The title, *UNDERGROUND RAILROAD, Harriet Tubman, Conductor,* popped out in bright colors and made no nonsense about slavery or the need for freedom. No one was sure whether Tubman ever actually came to Alton or Godfrey but she needed to show their connection to the UR. That picture was on the T-shirt and apron (though they came in different colors). Delphi and BrandyLee hoped that even though these were more souvenir-ish than their usual commodities a little more income might be generated and their cause forwarded. She also had some *Black Lives Matter* T-shirts and bracelets. BrandyLee Wilson was happy to be a Covid-survivor, though she had been sick for several weeks, apparently formed some anti-bodies from medication received. Not really sure just glad she's here because her g-g-grandma was one of the slaves that got saved by the UR and she loved to share *her-story*. BrandyLee knew it very well and the folks who came to visit wanted to know as well, reflected Delphi. Over in Godfrey they were preparing for the big visit, scheduling a band and some new vendors for an outdoor sale.

++

It was unlikely, Astra thought, that she would be the winner, wanting it so much! She was not sure what it was that drew her to Alton. She wanted to know. Of course, she could take the train on her own and study the UR. Conversely, all expenses paid sounded much better! Astra had finally concocted her recipe and tried it out on Beatrice, Percy and Alcor. So far so good. The judges were unknown for the first round but she'd find out tonight. Astra made sure she had her red hat, matching apron trimmed in red and casserole. She was ready to win.

7pm seemed to roar in like a healthy autumn wind. Beatrice had come to collect her and they were on their way out to the Parker Place. *Fig Fusion Sweet Potato Casserole*. Whadda name! Yup her dish was, well, you'll hear more later. Anyway, they got to the place and who do you think was a judge of this round? Nevaeh! Yes ma'am! She was older now, having left her tweens behind. She had no idea what Astra's casserole tasted like as she had been over at a friend's when the others were at Astra's kitchen. The other two judges were JasonMa and BobbyLou (from the quilt club).

Astra and Beatrice went to the registration desk where she got her number and instruction sheet. Number SEVEN was hers. There sat the *Fig Fusion* with just the number SEVEN, no names. They walked down the aisle, back up through the line of other tables and saw each one of the twenty-three entries with their number proudly displayed. A rather odd bell rang and all the folks visiting other vendors who wanted to see the judging came over. The contestants mixed into the crowd. No one knew who was who and to whom each casserole belonged. JasonMa welcomed everyone and explained how the judging would take place and that by the end of Friday evening they would have chosen the Final 4 bakers. The bake-off would be Saturday at 2pm and the Championship Final on Sunday at 3pm. They would announce the winner at 8pm during the dance. He also explained the Grand Prize (the Alton trip) and the runner-up prize, $100. Excitement was high. What a Feastival! The sisters were wandering around but their job was not until Sunday when just two contestants would present their casseroles. JasonMa encouraged everyone to visit the other vendors, said thanks and the music was returned to the max. Melodious was instantly in heaven.

++

Back in Alton Delphi was working hard to get the shop in order. It had originally been an old schoolhouse and her father, who inherited it from his father passed it down to her brother, who had died nearing eight years ago. She took it over and turned it into both an antique and modern art shop as well as highlighting some of the history of the area. Unlike BrandyLee who was black (from both parents) and could trace her slave heritage to the UR, Delphi was born of a white father and black mother both who came from Godfrey. She was fair but clearly favored her mother in bone structure and hair. Both parents had passed and even though people called her Mrs. she'd never married her intended who drown in the river one night. He was a handsome young black man and no one was ever sure just what happened. Delphi had her suspicions but in the day, those sorts of things were not very well investigated. Delphi was told he probably was fishing, didn't pay attention, or ran into a snake, fell in the water and was carried downstream on the hefty current. Possible reasons were offered by the police, with no evidence. End of story. Really? Frederick Moses hadn't gone fishing. She knew that. Frederick Moses had gone to the hardware store for fence building materials to surround the spot where they would build their new house the following year. He wanted to fence off the land to establish in a tangible way his property...soon to be their property. They intended to 'jump the broom' (as the old folks called it) within six months. Only one person had seen him at the hardware store and no one admitted seeing him leave there or head home. Frederick Moses never arrived. Nothing was found to tie anyone to a crime like bloody clothes, an eyewitness or anyone who would speak up. The local Sheriff did look around one afternoon down by the river and only found a part of an old boot (in the end it was not Frederick's) and some bits of an old cowboy hat, also not his. The Sheriff concluded that there was no crime just a tragic accident and the case was closed.

Delphi never recovered. How could you? Oh yes, she matured, worked and even continued to go to Church. (In fact, many years later she married Mr. Tom Spinach. Well that's another story...) She knew it was some of those Club boys who didn't even wear scary outfits anymore. There was one guy who very much hated Frederick Moses because Frederick Moses was a highly skilled carpenter and made quite a good salary for the 1950's. He had run-ins with him time and again, especially when trying to eat in the diner for locals. It wasn't illegal...just not 'encouraged'. Frederick Moses and Delphi paid as little attention as they might, often to no avail. The Club boys could be very wicked and houses burned. Wonder who did that? No evidence? No case. And on it went.

++

Some black folks traveled up from the depths of Mississippi over to the Underground Railroad to freedom. By 1840 the UR was running quite well, though the bounty hunters of 1835 around NYC had made it harder because there was so much money involved. However, on September 18, 1850 Congress passed the Fugitive Slave Act that created a force of Federal commissioners charged with returning escaped slaves to their owners. That meant that the UR and going North was a greater risk yet Canada was the real place folks wanted to go. Many made it. Many of the Northerners, through their own businesses were often complicit (to make their linen they needed cotton) tried in some cases to go to court and get the slaves freed. Sometimes it worked. Alton was right there on the MS River, just a few miles east of St. Louis and downriver from Hannibal where Mark Twain did a bit of writing.

The best BrandyLee could figure was that her g-g-g-grannie, Rose Amelia (would have been about 125 years old), was a picker of cotton in the Delta of the MS River near Greenville. From there she escaped her plantation and owner, eventually heading out for Memphis and Paducah, picking up her first conductors, crossing the Ohio River to Marion, Ill. They stayed close to the MS River up over to Belleville into Alton. Originally, she like many had been trying to get to that sweet spot on the Tennessee/Kentucky border where she could cross the Mason-Dixon line. On the way, she began to meet one conductor after another who took her in the Memphis direction.

At night, or costumed by day, she and two small children, JackBoy and Rosie (her g-grandma), ran to safety. It took them many days and they were grateful for the many stops they made in the homes, barns and hideouts of Quakers, abolitionists and others who were against slavery. One dusky evening though, while stashed in the cramped quarters of the false bottom of a carriage they came close to discovery. The lone driver was perhaps a bit careless. He jogged over the roads, hitting every pot -hole available, and she and the children cracked their heads with some force against the wooden frame, crying out just as he was going over a bridge into town. A man standing there heard the cries but saw no one and was just about to challenge the driver when his wife came and hurried him away. They were so close to their destination. One more trip and they would arrive near Alton, BrandyLee figured it was about 1855. Next, they were taken to a Quaker House and welcomed to the North. It was a night of joyous celebration. New clothes, a new place to live, her kids then seven and nine could grow up and not be slaves. Could anything be better? BrandyLee could trace the rest of what would become her family right down to her own mother. One of the treasures was a UR Quilt thought to have been designed and quilted by Rosie, g-g-g-grannie's daughter. BrandyLee had it hanging in the B&B because it was so amazing. It was part of the Civil War era quilts. They were happy to be in the North. How did she know all this? Her daughter (Rosie) passed the story down to her daughter (Amelia), down to her daughter Amelia Rose, and down to BrandyLee. Some stories were stitched into quilts, some simply written, and some was just plain old family oral tradition.

++

The Final 4 stood up and yes, Astra was one. Next was baking their entry right there in the barn, as would the Finalists on Sunday. The second set of judges would taste them and vote. That happened and yes, you guessed it, Astra was a semi-finalist with a young black man who'd only lived in the County four or five years. Frederick Mason-Dixon Godfrey was fine looking, a teacher at the elementary school, coaching the tiny basketball team and helping with the band. An all-rounder, his interests and skills were varied. Baking was at the top of his list. Frederick Mason-Dixon Godfrey stood tall and thoughtful in his apron of white. It looked like it had never seen a day's work in any kitchen. On it was stamped *EYE- BAKE: YEW- EAT.* Sunday would be both exciting and fraught for Astra and for him. He was nearly thirty (and single) and Astra was well, a bit over that. Frederick Mason-Dixon was #TWENTY-ONE. Astra wanted to get a good nights' sleep so she hitched a ride and went home to Dog and a hot cuppa. She mulled over in her mind the various strategies. Oh, pshaw, she almost grumbled, I don't need any strategies. I just need good fig jam, soft wonderful sweet potatoes from Vardaman, toasted coconut flakes and cornbread crumbs, a little of this and that. Well that will be the yummiest I've ever made. That is all I have to do. Just bake. Astra clicked out the lamp and was asleep before her eyelids closed. Dog snuggled in.

Sunday Astra went to Church (and not to Thee Café as usual). She figured she needed to center herself and give over to God everything about the competition. Astra was just glad to be participating and the money raised from the contest was going to repurpose and renovate the school cafeteria and improve the menu. The Elementary kids would be overjoyed, though they loved those chicken nuggets. The High Schoolers would appreciate some choices in the fruit and vegetable department, not over -cooked with lots of salt, actually not cooked at all, fresh out of local farms and gardens. Astra also prayed for Frederick Mason-Dixon Godfrey her competitor.

Beatrice, dressed in her favorite brown corduroy blazer and smart loafers (a bit dated but so comfortable), collected Astra after Church and off they went to the Parkers Place barn where she'd left all her equipment, ingredients, and apron. Astra was ready. Or so she thought. The baking would begin at 3pm BUT when she arrived most of Astra's ingredients were missing. Gone. No. Can't be. Secured on Saturday night by herself and an aide and then the barn was locked. Where could they be? Frederick Mason-Dixon had arrived and all his stuff seemed in order. He came over to talk to her. She had taken to sitting down on a rather rickety chair near the stove.

"What happened?" he asked with great gentleness.

"I have no idea. You look around maybe you will find them? It's just the ingredients. My other stuff is here."

Frederik Mason-Dixon did just that and came back with a somber face. "Yup missing. Nowhere to be found," he declared. "What to do now?"

Beatrice came over to see if she could lend a hand. The sisters were already promenading around (loving their judges t-shirts) and they too came by to check on the contestants. One look at Astra and they knew something was wrong. She explained it all and Beatrice decided there and then to hive off to *SuperBuy* and get the missing stuff. Only one tickly problem, the key ingredient, the rich fig jam made by her friend was not in the store. They needed to go to her home and get a jar, hoping she had not given it all away by now. Beatrice phoned Emila who was happy to have just finished an even better batch. All the other ingredients including the cornbread mix, the pecans, and the coconut (to be toasted) were in stock at *SuperBuy*. They shopped with focus and were out in less than half an hour, arriving back at the barn around 2:30pm, to sit down just for a few minutes before the competition began.

Frederick Mason-Dixon was delighted to see them back and though he had a lot of his own work to do, he was glad things had resolved. Well not exactly and you might find this hard to believe but the ingredients were never discovered. Not a whiff of fig jam or toasted coconut flakes, nor cornbread crumbs for the toasting anywhere to be found. Ever. It was 3pm, and JasonMa took the mic and gathered people round the two bakers.

"I am so happy y'all are here at our autumn Feastival and we are now going to get underway for the last time. At the end of the baking period the judges, our wonderful three sisters (they blushed as they bowed) are going to find just the right one to be the winner. We know it is going to be close because both of these skilled bakers have charmed us before. Of course, the judges, I remind you, will not know who baked which casserole until the winner is chosen, and the card turned over. Big mystery upcoming. Bakers, I know you have had a great time in this competition and I ask that you take great care in your final presentation." They both smiled at him from their place behind their kitchen's island and gave a little wave. "Finally, I just want to thank all twenty-three entrants and their wonderful contribution to our Feastival. So far we've raised $32,000 for our project. You still have time to donate at the dance tonight . Bakers are you ready?" They smiled again, shook hands and awaited JasonMa's bell and direction '*gitter done*!' The baking began. The wonderful aroma of both their casseroles soon began to fill the barn and folks were looking forward to a taste!

That was a dream deferred because when the baking was concluded, Melodious, Sarahfina, and Whiplash began judging. That meant tasting each one, well, was *one* taste of each really enough, they wondered? No way, so another taste and very soon both casseroles were gone! The sisters ate the lot! Finally, they did decide the winner and turned over the card…

All the decorations were in place for the big barn dance. The square dancers were prancing around in their cowboy clothes, the round dancers in knee pants and long socks, and the hip-hoppers were tuning up their boxes of magic for some demonstration dancing as well as for everyone to try. The confluence of music was a cacophony and one might actually want to hold hands over ears for a while (unless you were Melodious. She was sure she'd died and gone to heaven!)! Vendors still had their goods available and as folks began to come in for the dance, they were still able to shop. The donation jars continued to fill. Heaps of wonderful handcrafted goods, as well as homemade jams and jellies, fruitcakes, pies, and the lot remained. It was not too early to begin holiday shopping. There was even Mark & Marcie's marble table. Oh, they had some beauties. Nevaeh had been over there many times and was still basking in the glorious trip she had with Beatrice over to Alabama where he taught her how to make a glass marble. The crowd over the weekend had swelled and the vendors did very well. That was always a good sign. When the local County folk supported it well others come from miles around. The dance was the only activity that had a fee, $5 single or $8 couple and that money would also go to the cafeteria project. It was 7:30pm. Frederick Mason-Dixon and Astra were sitting off in a corner talking with one another about their casseroles.

"Mine is called *Fig Fusion*" Astra told him. "I was lucky enough to get some of my friend's newest fig jam (with a touch of clove) and I think it the yummiest I've made; mixed with the softest of sweet potatoes, and covered with toasted coconut flakes, pecans, and cornbread crumbs, I think it's mighty tasty. I use a bit of cool-whip, or ice cream depending upon preference. Your syrup idea sounds de-lish!"

Frederick Mason-Dixon smiled. "Mine is an *Apple Crisp*. Besides the very finely sliced Granny Smith apples layered with the mashed sweet potatoes (also from Vardaman) and lots of brown sugar when it's served you put just a bit of sorghum syrup on it and maybe a bit of cool whip. De-lish indeed!"

"Oh that sounds so good I look forward to having a taste. I'll be glad when this is over though. I'm a bit bushed. What do you think of the trip up to Alton, ILL? If I win, I would like you to go with me. Would you? You might learn a lot about that area and the UR. You are originally from St. Louis aren't you?"

Frederick Mason-Dixon looked at her with amazement. "Why, well, of course, if you like. It's a weekend I think in late October and so I'd not be teaching. Yes, I was born there but moved here to MS when I was two, actually to Jackson State, where both my parents got their teaching credentials. We lived in a little country place near Raymond. I moved to this County almost five years ago to accept this teaching job. I did some study at Jackson State, Mississippi State and 'Ole Miss. I have a MEd and one-day hope to do a PhD in School Administration. Maybe I could become a Superintendent? My dad is still teaching over in North Carolina. In fact, I think my grandfather lives somewhere near Alton."

"Gosh, those are some impressive qualifications and I'd love to hear more! Where did you study culinary arts? As far as the trip, well see I will need a bit of help getting around and we have been through so much together I'd like to share it. But, we'll see. I have not won yet!" They both laughed.

"I guess I taught myself mostly. I love to eat and so did my parents. They often had long after-school stuff going and so I'd cook our meals. I'm an only child."

It was nearing 8pm and the music went down to a gentle rumble. JasonMa and the three sisters went to the podium. He rang his funny little bell and called the barn to attention.

"Ladies and gents, we have a winner! The winner of this year's Autumn Feastival Sweet Potato Casserole Competition is…there was deafening, exacting and exciting silence, Astra and Frederick Mason-Dixon were holding hands…wait for it is ASTRA FISIC, our slightly retired astronomer, and there she is under her red hat, in her red trimmed apron!!!" He pointed at Astra who had struggled just a bit to stand. The barn-folk collapsed in oooohs, ahahas, clapping and hugging. Frederick Mason-Dixon reached over and hugged Astra and she hugged back. They both went to the podium where JasonMa said very marvelous things about Frederick's *Apple Crisp Sweet Potato Casserole*, gave him a runner-up ribbon, and $100 check. He beamed and thanked people, told them how glad he was to have been a finalist and that he was so proud to teach in this County. Folks applauded again. He moved off to the left of the podium and JasonMa called Astra Fisic to the center. "Astra, you and your *Fig Fusion Sweet Potato Casserole* have wowed the judges to the extent that they ate the whole thing." He looked over at Frederick Mason-Dixon and said, "And they ate all of yours as well!" Folks cheered and laughed. The sisters flushed a bit but knew they could not possibly have made a good decision if they had not tasted enough. The people were agreeable and wanted copies of the recipes.

Astra beamed at Frederick Mason-Dixon Godfrey and knew they were in for quite a trip.

"Congratulations and here is your grand prize winner ribbon and the ticket to the <u>Underground Railway Tour</u> in Alton, ILL, in October. And your train ticket. All expenses are paid. You will leave on the 21st from Jackson in a night sleeper train to St. Louis and then a car will meet you and take you to Alton's *SingingBird* B&B where you will stay. The 22-24th will be the tours and whatever else and then travel back on the 25th. How does that sound?"

"Well, it sounds incredible and wonderful and after I take a nap or two I'll be ready to travel. It's only September 25 today so I'll be ready." Astra was drained and very chuffed. "I want to say that I have invited young Mr. Frederick Mason-Dixon to attend me and so we will be traveling together. I wanted to share this with him. And besides he's got another $100 we can spend!" The audience hooted, generous with their applause.

"Sounds like a great idea to me," someone from the crowd yelled out. "We'll look forward to hearing all about it when y'all git back!" With that the music picked up and the square dancer's caller was ready to go. Frederick Mason-Dixon and Astra decided to give it a miss. "I'm sorta tuckered out," he said. "Think I'll finish loading up my gear and head for home. You?"

"Me too," Astra said as she perused the crowd looking for someone to take her home. "Would you mind giving me a ride? I don't see my folks. I think they're very involved with dancing." "Pleasure," his face lit up. "Let's boogie!" And off they went in his white SUV.

The month passed quickly and Astra and Frederick Mason-Dixon were busy packing. Beatrice had agreed to take them down to Jackson to the train. Nevaeh wanted to go too. Frederick Mason-Dixon had never been back to the St. Louis area so it was all new for him. Maybe he'd see his grandfather after all these years? What great adventure for a history buff. Astra had been to Chicago but never over that way to St. Louis.

++

Astra loved the train ride and she and Frederick Mason-Dixon appreciated each other even more. Their sleepers were right next to each other and the porters stowed their luggage. Astra got her stuff organized and loved talking to Christopher who was there to settle her in. He explained about coming back at whatever time she wanted and fixing her bed. Christopher also explained she could order food from him, eat here or go up to the dining car. He would let her know in time. Astra was fascinated and very happy. Frederick Mason-Dixon got the same little lesson from the other porter on their car, Ronald. When Frederick Mason-Dixon set up house, he went out, locked the door and knocked on Astra's door.

"Hey, there," he called. Astra answered, "Come on in, the door ain't locked." And in he rolled, where he found a secure place to sit and they just relaxed for over half an hour, watching out the window at the trees and farms, little towns and traffic that whizzed by. They bounced up and down a bit. It was as if the train was the whole world and everything surrounding it or approaching it had to stop so that it might barrel on.

"What's for dinner?" Frederick Mason-Dixon asked.

"Don't know but I'm getting hungry. Christopher said to ring this bell if I wanted anything. Let's do it and get a menu. Do you want to eat in dining car or here?"

"I'd be happy to eat right here. You?"

"Perfect"

Astra pushed the little button and within ten minutes Christopher was knocking on her door.

"Here's yer menus," he said, handing them each one. "I'll be back in another ten minutes, or I can take it now?"

"Now would be perfect," they spoke it together and snapped their fingers. Both quickly perused the menus and ordered. Frederick Mason-Dixon decided on a light beer and so did Astra. Nice and cold. Christopher returned with their meals after half an hour and they ate like they were starving. Both had ordered the rib-eye steak with all the trimmings, salad, and veg. For dessert, he had blueberry pie (hot) with ice cream and Astra had a flan. (It is nice, Astra thought, when all expenses are paid!)

"I think it's time to fix my bed," she said dreamily. "I need to sleep tonight. Whadda 'bout you?"

"I think I'll go up to the lounge car and see what I can see for a while. I'll send Christopher down to help out. You know where the bathroom is?"

"Yes, Christopher showed me. In fact, that's my next destination."

Frederick Mason-Dixon departed, climbed the twist of stairs and found a seat in the middle of the car. The sky was dark, almost as dark as it was going to get that night. He could see loads of stars when they were passing through the fields. Light shone off in tiny towns and by train trellises and warning spots. The stars were clear but hard to see through scratched windows.

He was a very interesting young man and she was so glad he was a teacher. Our elementary kids need male teachers, black male teachers, young teachers who can reach right down and bring education to the slowest, the fastest, the 'regulars'. Not such an easy task these days, she thought.

"I don't know all that much about the UR," he told her. "I really want to learn because in my fifth and sixth grade history classes this is going to be like gold. I intend to photograph and video all our tours!" he had told her during dinner.

"Well," Astra said, "I hope to do some of the same but I'm actually interested in how the slaves got on *after* they got there. I'm looking forward to talking to a woman called Delphi Spinach. Her name's about as weird as mine! She and her co-worker, BrandyLee have set up a couple of times to talk to me and you'd be welcome to join us."

The night was not motionless but it was free from accidents or adventures. Both slept and awakened just as the sun was peeping into their windows. Christopher was knocking on Astra's door, asking what she wanted for breakfast and having brought along a strong cup of de-café, with just a little cream, he would forever be in her hero book. Ronald was helping Frederick Mason-Dixon. They ate breakfast in her sleeper, cleared up, re-packed and talked for the next three hours. Tiny towns with little dinging bells would forever remain imprinted in their brains. Railway arms blocked the traffic as their train sped by. It was a glorious ride.

++

"Not long now until we get into St. Louis." They arrived on time and the car was awaiting them, the driver holding a large sign over his head: ASTRA FISIC & FREDERICK MASON-DIXON.

"Well, that's us," Frederick Mason-Dixon said and they moved toward the red mini-van, needing to get their luggage. The driver took their tickets after seating them and was back in a flash. All packed up and ready to go they set out for the final leg of their UR into Alton.

"That feeling I'm having," Astra began, "is what some of those poor people must have been feeling, just hoping the last little bit wouldn't mess them up!"

"Yea, I'm having a bit of that myself," Frederick Mason-Dixon agreed.

The driver had introduced himself as Mr. Garland Wiles of the URCompany. "I am so happy to meet y'all (is that what you'd say in the South?). I hope the next few days will be so enlightening and encouraging. I hear y'all won a contest?"

163

"Yes, it was a Sweet Potato Casserole, believe it or not, at our County Autumn Harvest Feastival. We decided we both won so here we are together!" Astra beamed.

"Well, that sounds wonderful. A *Feast*ival. Now that's clever! Ah, here we are now at the *SingingBird* B&B where you will be staying." Mr. Wiles drove carefully onto the gravel parking lot, the wheels crunching and scraping along, and edged up to the delivery point. Standing in the path was a very attractive black woman smiling from ear to ear her arms outstretched. She looked so excited and welcoming.

"I'm BrandyLee," she announced and you must be Astra and Frederick Mason-Dixon. We are so glad you are both here. Cum'on in to the *SingingBird*. May I show you around and to your rooms? Maybe y'all would like something to eat or drink?"

Astra and Frederick Mason-Dixon smiled back, handled their own hand luggage and followed BradyLee and Mr. Wiles into the B&B. Oh, it was quaint and beautiful; so cozy and comfortable. Astra replied she'd love a cuppa tea and a lie down before any of the other instructions were given so she might remember what was said! Mr. Wiles took his leave. Frederick Mason-Dixon had tried to tip him but was gently reminded that 'all expenses were paid.' The open front room was full of upside-down roses drying on a long piece of twine strung across the sidewall. They must have been gorgeous and full, Astra thought, and now saved by this simple process. There were two couches and two recliners (both generously equipped with fleece throws) and she could just see herself sitting in one and dozing off (though she did miss Dog). There was a rather patriotic area rug in the center with various birds encircling a USA flag. It fit over a clearly older rug with a weave Astra found interesting. The edges weren't very wide but she could appreciate what she saw. The curtains were light and full of yellows, yellow checks, yellow flowers, and yellow bees. Yes bees. Soon she would discover the hives out in the back and taste the bees' careful work on her biscuits and waffles. There was an older pattern of wallpaper with 'family' photos along the passageway to her room and as she moved across the big living room, the UR Civil War Quilt was brightly displayed along the front wall. Astra didn't know the pattern though she thought it might contain a North Star map. BrandyLee would tell her all about it she hoped and if not Delphi Spinach might. Later she would take pics and be sure to send to her quilt club members. Beatrice would spare no expense at discovery of any information needed.

"Of course, I'll bring it right up, unless you want to crash here?" BrandyLee said with a gentle smile realizing Astra's exhaustion. Astra demurred. Frederick Mason-Dixon wasn't that tired, declined a cup of tea, and thought he'd go out and walk around. "Dinner will be at 5:30pm. It's about 3pm now so may I call for you around five so you have time to freshen up?" Astra thought that a very good plan.

BrandyLee had owned the *SingingBird Inn* for about five years in partnership with Mrs. Spinach who owned *SpinachSpecialties* and *HealthFood Store*. It was BrandyLee's idea to do the tours again and Delphi was excited to participate in the first one.

Astra was delighted, slipped off her shoes, slacks and sweater and crashed onto the wonderful bed full of quilts and wonderful fragrances. Frederick Mason-Dixon had already slipped out but heard the word 'dinner'. He'd be there, for sure! Astra slept for over two hours and awakened to the cup of tea she had forgotten to drink. Obviously, it was cold, but tasted quite nice. Had a very flavorful spice in it, not sure which one but possibly sassafras (she recognized the root beer taste). She sat up on the bed, ruffled her hair, and looked for her slacks. The room had two windows out onto the lovely landscape. One pointed toward the rose garden and the other looked out over a little creek and bridge. The soft rocker sat in front of the creek window and she plunked down with her notebook. I need to write down all my questions for Mrs. Spinach, she reminded herself; our meeting is after dinner around 7pm.

Dinner was a wonderful thick beef stew with lots of tender beef, potatoes and vegetables, a salad, rolls, and drink of your choice. Dessert was luscious thick hot apple pie with warm cheddar cheese.

"I was hungrier than I thought," Astra admitted to Frederick Mason-Dixon, who was already having seconds of the stew and salad. "You?"

"Well as you can see *eyes jess a po growin' boy needin' a lottsa food ta hep me!*" They chuckled. "BrandyLee said our Tour starts tomorrow at 9am. Breakfast (and she encouraged us not to miss it) is a buffet between 6:30am and 8:30am. Whaddya think? She mentioned another person would be joining us along with these three other couples. Didn't say who it was but thought we would enjoy the person's presence."

"If I go off to bed just now I'll sleep the deepest and I'll be ready whenever you are. I won't be bobbing up and down but I will miss that train whistle as we passed through all those little towns. Breakfast at what 7:45am? Oh no I can't go to bed yet, not quite yet, she eked out, feeling a bit scrambled. I have a meeting at 7pm with Mrs. Spinach first. Wanna come?"

"Yea, OK, I have a few questions myself! Sounds good to me. I had a little walk-about while you were napping. You're gonna love this place!" Frederick Mason-Dixon had discovered a sort of bulletin board with interesting postings. There he caught sight of a list of persons: Frederick Mason Godfrey, Frederick George Godfrey, Frederick Alan Godfrey, and Frederick Mason-Dixon Godfrey. It was his name, right there on that list. Really? The names fell under a sign marked: INFORMATION NEEDED ABOUT…Frederick Mason-Dixon was very surprised and wondered, what in the world??? He thought to inquire with BrandyLee the next day. He would wait until then; or maybe Mrs. Spinach would know tonight?

++

Mrs. Delphi Spinach glided into the far front room and welcomed Astra and Frederick Mason-Dixon. She was right on time. 7pm. They had comfortably selected the recliners and Mrs. Spinach headed for the cozy love seat nearby, upholstered with needlepoint, as were many of the chairs, the piano stool, and some pillows. Beautiful work, wonder who's it was?

"I am so happy you both came. I was hoping you would."

"How would you know there might be two?" Astra inquired gently.

"Well," Mrs. Spinach said, "these are just some of the things I know. She tapped her nose and smiled. Her bright dark almost black eyes twinkled and her cornrowed nappy silver hair was in a beautiful design.

"Now I know you've not been here but five minutes but we both have lots of questions." Astra and Frederick Mason-Dixon looked at each other and over at her. Astra was feeling a bit, well, wary of Mrs. Spinach (who asked to be called Delphi mostly). Who was this woman? Her shawl was dangling around her bony shoulders, the metallic threads popped in the evening light, over her off-white linen blouse. Her long skirt was a quilt pattern of some sort and gently fell to her ankles. Then there were Delphi's boots. She had on a pair of genuine soft American, Texas USA cowboy boots with the hand-painted impression of a river winding around from top to bottom. Truthfully, they seemed worn out, though they looked sturdy enough for tonight. Delphi's fingers were long and beautiful, her nails shone in the evening light and her wireless glasses slid down her nose just a bit. The meeting was very productive. Frederick Mason-Dixon and Astra went off to bed hoping that more information was to come. The one thing Astra would remember was something about a ring. She was not so sure Frederick Mason-Dixon heard that part.

Could the breakfast buffet have served anything else? That was Frederick Mason-Dixon's question as he dove in. Most everything one imagines (maybe not dinosaur steaks) was served. Astra had waffles with sugar-free syrup and pecans. Frederick Mason-Dixon, adventurer that he was, tried a bit of everything. That included those very fatty but scrumptious polish sausages, the crispest bacon going, some scrambled eggs, one little waffle (with lots of honey), and who knows what else. Astra topped hers off with some sliced fruit and a small piece of cheddar cheese (made in Wisconsin) and a cup of strong de-cafe. "Oh, my," she groaned. "Will I be able to stroll as we go?" Frederick Mason-Dixon told her about the list on the board. She was very curious indeed. "Why didn't you ask Delphi last night?"

"Not sure but I am a bit shy and thought I'd wait for just the right moment. Those three other names are my father, grandfather, and g-g-father. See my mom is black and my father white. She was from Alton and he was from Godfrey. When they married she became an 'Alton-Godfrey'." He munched on through another waffle and a very large cup of black coffee whose aroma filled the room.

"We'll have to ask BrandyLee when we see her at 3pm. Our tour returns around twelve for lunch. I propose a nap following!" Astra had that quirky look she often unmasked when she cocked her head and began to laugh. Frederick Mason-Dixon smiled, placed his hand on her bony shoulder and agreed. They set off for the mini-van.

Mr. Garland Wiles of URCompany was smartly dressed in company bow tie, cap, and vest monogrammed with URC. He rolled up into the parking lot, crunching the gravel under the wheels and inviting the folks into the beautiful recently purchased red hot mini-van. There were six adventurers: Beth and Ken, a young married couple from California, Sarah from South Dakota, Veronique from France (who spoke very good English) and, of course, Astra and Frederick Mason-Dixon. The van was a seven seater, well, eight if you included Garland's. Homely like the rest of their hospitality; relaxing though a bit nip and tuck. There was room for one more. Frederick Mason-Dixon whispered in Astra's ear about who he thought it might be. Would he be correct?

Looked like a marvelous day, the clouds very high in a very blue sky. There wasn't much wind but somewhere nearby someone was burning slash or a new campfire. The smoke was not oppressive (as it had been in California just the previous year) but lent that *fall y'all* feeling to the trip. Leaves of various colors, especially oranges from crusty browns, and a few yellows blew off the trees and onto the pavement. There were still some greens staying stuck to the middle branches; they would not last forever. Some had wonderful designs on them and Astra meant to collect some before they left for Mississippi. Mr. Wiles (said to call him Garland) was ready to roll. Just as he was turning the van toward the parking lot exit he heard:

"Wait for me, wait for me." It was Mrs. Spinach hurrying across the parking lot. "So sorry I'm almost late, but don't want to miss this!" Garland stopped, got out and gently assisted her into the van, finding the last empty seat, right next to Frederick Mason-Dixon and Astra. They greeted each other warmly and Delphi and Astra picked up where they had left off the evening before. Frederick Mason-Dixon winked at Astra, had he guessed right?

"Everybody belted in? Ready to ride?" he chuckled. Folks played along, "Yes sir!" So was he. He placed his hat on the top of the dashboard, put on his metallic blue mirror sunglasses, and turned on the mic. "First we are going over to visit a little museum that depicts the maps and other memorabilia of the Underground Railway. Will give you a little background and there is a fifteen minute video. Finishing that Ms. Bell, the proprietor, will answers questions. We have found them to be the best information hub around and I hope you will enjoy it." Garland requested seatbelts (again), no smoking in the mini-van, and prompt return to the van when finished. Sounded a bit like a conductor! "Oh," he asked, "have you been to the National UR Freedom Center in downtown Cincinnati?" No one had perhaps it would show up on their *ta do* list?

169

The trip over to the UR Museum and Gift Shop only took half an hour so Frederick Mason-Dixon and Astra chatted with Mrs. Spinach and he asked her about the list. "I feel a bit like I'm on a FBI Most Wanted!" he said with some alarm. "What in the world? Why who'd know I'd ever come here anyway? And why are my father, grandfather, and g-grandfather also listed?" Astra calmly suggested that maybe the list didn't go up until BrandyLee knew you were coming? "Anyway," she said, "I suspect it has to be good news." Mrs. Spinach was not sure about the list but knew it had been there over six months, long before the winners of that little contest in far- away Mississippi would produce Mr. Frederick Mason-Dixon Godfrey.

Frederick Mason-Dixon looked at Astra and queried, "Did you know anything about this? I mean is this why you invited me to come along?"

"Nope. Nada. Notta hint. I was coming, I found out, to meet Mrs. Spinach and am so pleased to be doing just that. Maybe this is all tied up together?" Astra turned to Delphi and gave her an inquiring look. Delphi smiled back, tapping the right side of her nose and snapping her fingers.

The river was in sight and a beautiful river it was. Astra kept thinking how much it must have cost a person to jump in (after all that riding and hiding in various places under a variety of transport) and just well, take that last chance for freedom. Musta cost everything within them; especially if they had small children. Seems one would have to shut off the mind where fears and worries shot through, and do it midst just downright being scared. And if you didn't swim well, ooops maybe this wasn't the place to cross!

The first tour went beautifully and all were glad to get home for lunch, a wee nap, and an afternoon of storytelling. The second tour took them into the Middletown Historical District, the very wealthy area of Henry and East 12th Streets, over by the Victorian Playhouse, and eventually back by the Rocky Forth Church (1816, the first 'free' stop for UR riders). The tours were about two hours each and though relaxing they were challenging. Both (and perhaps the others in the van) were trying to get their heads around a concept and indeed a practice called: slavery where one person could actually own another, like owning a horse. It is not as if they hadn't studied it in school a bit, but here they felt faced with the reality. They inspected the 1830's AME Church, another important stop on the rails. Frederick Mason-Dixon was even more concerned about his discovery. They only had another full day and a half to go and there must be something for him to learn. He had set up a meeting with BrandyLee for 4pm and Astra would join them.

++

"Well, Mr. Godfrey, I have to tell you that if you are able to match my information, I am going to pass you on to your grandfather! We were astonished to discover he had in his possession a 'treasure' and the only way we could verify its authenticity was our tried and true oral history. We thought we would need your father and grandfather at least and sure enough this 'treasure' lies with your grandfather, Frederick Mason Godfrey. He wanted to be sure that it got passed on to you before he died, and though he is still with us over in Godfrey, when he heard you were coming our way, he thought he would pass it along now."

Frederick Mason-Dixin stared at BrandyLee, what in the world could it be?

She asked him several questions, all answered to suit her. "Do you want to phone your g-father now and set up a visit for this evening?"

"Yes, well, OK, whatever works. Can Astra come?"

"Of course. I'll be right back with the number."

She returned, they phoned and would go over to Frederick Mason's house around 7pm.

Dinner came and went and Mr. Wiles, BrandyLee, and Delphi escorted Astra and Frederick Mason-Dixon over across town and for several miles to Godfrey and Mr. Frederick Mason's home. All along from the beginning of the contest Astra thought it was about her or some distant relative in her family, but surprise surprise! It was all about Frederick's long family ties and a 'treasure'. Who would have thought that baking a sweet potato casserole would open up US History in such a bold and vivid way, to say nothing of his own family? Who wouldda thought?

There was a little white picket fence around the small lawn of Mr. Frederick Mason Godfrey's house. He was standing under the porch light awaiting their arrival. He'd not seen his grandson for about twenty years when he went South to see his son's family before they moved to North Carolina. Apparently, there were some kinks in the relationships and though no one knew for sure it had to do with the 'treasure' the family had thought about for many many years. Frederick Alan Godfrey thought it should have come to him, not to his son (Frederick Mason-Dixon). Anyway, folks get it in their heads that this or that is the whole story and things get mixed up and then folks quit talking and then… well, you know. Whatever it was the old man was cranky and unhappy about it all so when he heard Frederick Mason-Dixon was coming to town he decided to make the hand-off. Would another sore spot be created as his son was still living in North Carolina? He hoped Frederick Mason-Dixon would be the generation to sort it out.

Astra, sensing the tension, walked right up to him and struck out her hand, "So nice to meet you! We've come a far way to hear all about this 'treasure'!" He was a little astonished but thrust out his hand for the shake. His grandson stood behind her and did the same when he let go of Astra. Delphi followed as did BrandyLee and Mr. Wiles. They followed him into the sitting room filled with the lovely aroma of coffee . Though the room was small, there were plenty of seats and he graciously invited them to find one. He asked Frederick Mason-Dixon to sit next to him. The coffee and lovely coffee-cake would come later.

"I don't really know what you know or don't know," he turned to Frederick Mason-Dixon. "Stories down family rails often get confused and certainly argued about one generation after another. So I'm going to tell y'all the story I know." Frederick Mason-Dixon had never heard *any* of the story. Folks smiled and awaited the moment. BrandyLee though not part of the family was, as a historian, very interested.

"During the Civil War your g-g-g- grandfather Frederick George Mason Godfrey (would be about 124 years old) fought for the South. He had a son, Frederick George Godfrey (would be 104 years) who had a son Frederick Mason Godfrey (that's me I'm 84 years old) and I had a son, Frederick Alan Godfrey (who is 59) who married SUZIEMAE ALTON (who is black). They had a son, Frederick Mason-Dixon Godfrey (and you are nearly 30)." Frederick Mason-Dixon smiled. "Whew! That's either very confusing or so clarifying."

"Slaves ran away in some cases (the UR tells some of that tale) others were returned to owners and chained, others went to the Army. As well young white folks did just that. He was sixteen they say, but a boy. He got home safely after the War and worked in whatever kind of work he could find. After he married and had his son, he began a story about a 'treasure' he had brought back from the War. He got home just after 1863. When he died, his son inherited it. No one ever saw what exactly it was until he had his son and I decided to show it around. Even then no one was quite sure what it was until a woman I met at the University, an anthropologist and Civil War memorabilia expert put me onto it." He turned and looked at Frederick Mason-Dixon. "Son, here is the 'treasure'." He took a small well-crafted wooden box out of his drawer in the little table near him and gave it to his grandson. "Go ahead open it and see if you can tell what it is."

Frederick Mason-Dixon did just that. The rest were straining their heads a bit trying to see. Slowly he opened the box and peeled back the worn satin material. It was a ring. He took it out and laid it in the palm of his hand. If it went all the way back to 1863 it was still amazingly shiny and in very good shape."

"Know what it is?" his grandfather asked.

"Not really except the obvious. But for a ring it has a bit of an odd shape. Would anyone actually wear it?"

His grandfather smiled and said, "You're on to it, son. Yes, it was worn but maybe not as you would expect. It is a ring forged and hammered from a link of chain worn around the neck of a human person, a slave." They had all been holding their breath and when he spoke they exhaled together, like a choir. Eyes popped and looks of amazement were all around.

"According to the story of my grandfather, his grandfather, Frederick George Mason came upon it when he met a man at a market somewhere around Birmingham when he was leaving the South to move back here to Godfrey. The man said he had created it, having found several links of chain thrown to the side of the road, picked them up put them in his pack and carried them to his home where he was a blacksmith. There he decided to do something with them. This was authentic, he swore, as he was the man who had made this. So my father bought it and made the man write his name on a paper and put the date on it. 1863. That paper has gone missing in the midst of it all but my g- father swore he remembered what the man wrote for Frederick George Mason."

Frederick Mason-Dixon passed it around for each one to hold and consider. Frederick Mason got up and brought out the coffee and coffee cake. Silence reigned. The rest of the visit was small talk compared to what had been revealed and what they held in their hands, and as it turned to 10:30pm, they decided to head out. Frederick Mason wrapped the ring back up and gave the box to Frederick Mason-Dixon with a hug. "Do show it to your father, I know he's over in North Carolina but the next time you see him" he said, "tell him there was nothing personal in giving it to you rather than him. He would have had to give it to you one day anyway." Frederick Mason-Dixon assured him he would though he thought it strange it didn't go to his father Frederick Alan first. They trekked out into the darkness toward the bright red van, turning to wave good-bye, and were nearly asleep when they returned to Alton.

++

The train rumbled along taking them South and back home to Mississippi. Astra and Frederick Mason-Dixon chatted and every now and then took out the ring and marveled at how the artist had turned such a horrid thing into something rather beautiful. They had discovered engraved on the inside of the ring *freedom*. Astra never heard the part about Frederick Mason-Dixon and his Dad so we can't tell that. What we can tell is how families often have to take risks to value the story of another and to respect their hopes and dreams. About a year later, she did hear that his g-father, Frederick Mason died up in Godfrey. Frederick Mason-Dixon went up to the funeral with his father Frederick Alan and they were able to heal a few of the rips and tears that come with living an estranged life. His father told him he had never seen the 'treasure' nor heard much of the story. He was glad his father had given it to Frederick Mason-Dixon and wanted him to keep it for his child. Astra stayed in contact with her new friend Delphi and ordered things from BrandyLee's shop.

++

Astra's red hat had survived the trip though Delphi tried to get her to part with it. She found another quite like it and sent it as a thank you for the wonderful time.

++

Sunday morning, Thee Café, before Church; why the place was full including Frederick Mason-Dixon. Even Burger was quietly sitting next to Officer Marvin awaiting their many amazing stories of the trip to Alton & Godfrey. Tall stacks all around with blueberry jam, and honey from Delphi's bees. Frederick Mason-Dixon began by telling all that he'd met his grandfather Frederick Mason Godfrey for only the second time. "He had a whole history of my family to tell me, well us," he went on, "and I have something to share." Holding up a little wooden box for all to see he asked them to guess what just might be in it...

THE END

12

Astra Fisic and the Herald of Good News

Astra Fisic, our slightly retired astronomer with the red hat is about four weeks away from Christmas. During Advent, she will pray and fast (a little bit) and find ways to celebrate. Her trip in late October with Frederick Mason-Dixon to Alton, Ill. had been amazing. Rolling back South on the train and in some discussion with him, you remember he is an elementary teacher, they explored her topic for the Christmas lecture: *The Christmas Star.* She wanted her talk to touch the reality that Christmas matters; that Jesus matters! She wanted folks to know that the Star showed even Gentiles where the Messiah was born! As an astronomer, Astra understood well the contrasts of light and darkness so accepting the invitation to give the Christmas Lecture at '*the dogwood*' was a focus of her preparation during Advent.

++

Sunday morning at Thee Café with her friends, Astra tried to negotiate through a bit of a bust- up between Melodious and Whiplash. You might remember that Melodious, the one in the middle is tone-deaf,

62, and loves okra swimming in a pot of stew and that Whiplash is the eldest, 65, and very accident-prone loves game pie, full-o-possum. Now that's not the problem, just letting you in on where they're coming from. (Sarahfinna, their other sister, 59, the youngest, has an acidic stomach and loves fried squirrel, was absent).

Anyway, when Astra got to Thee Café for her Sunday morning visit and breakfast (tall-stack and apple butter) there was a din of noise and everyone was watching Whiplash and Melodious squabble.

"Yes, you did," Melodious squeaked. "Yes, you did. My wallet was right here and you took it! Yes, you did!"

"I did not," Whiplash tried to say quietly in under 100 clean words. "I did not...why would I take your wallet? I have my own and my own money and do not need yours! You must have lost it or left it at the farm?" her voice softened and she tried to de-escalate the situation.

"*Why* would I leave it there when I knew we were coming to breakfast?" Melodious snapped sarcastically.

"Well, I don't really know, but unless you have a better answer than me stealing it from you..."

Melodious burst into tears.

Whiplash looked over and saw Astra coming in the door stepping on the easily- tripped -over rubber rug. She knew as she frequently did it!

"Ugh, this woman is going to drive me zany! She says I stole her wallet. Now just why would I do that?" Whiplash, looking over at Astra pleaded, becoming a bit more frantic for all the audience.

Astra looked at these supposedly mature women and then she looked around at all the other folks looking at them. "Girls, girlfriends," she began, "whaddya doin' ? It's Sunday morning, let's eat! Then we're gonna pray. There must be a very simple answer."

The grumpy sisters shouted back, "We've eaten. We're leavin!"

"Well, I just got here and thought we were to discuss our plans about Christmas and such. Are you really going to leave?"

"Yes." And they did, but not without Whiplash having to pay for them both, leaving her very testy and Melodious equally irritable. They even had to travel home together (unusual) as Melodious had no license with her. She would return later to collect her car if she found her wallet.

Astra left Thee Café and went over to visit Beatrice after such a weird, goofy, and very disheartening breakfast spectacle. She sat down at the kitchen table and looked at Beatrice who was futzing about making coffee and toast. When she told her the story they decided to leave it be! Stay out of other people's business. They continued sharing pictures and laughs that came from their summer trip around Mississippi and New Orleans.

"Look at this one, *Café de Monde* in New Orleans. You've got powdered sugar all over your face. Reminds me of when the biscuit container exploded and I had pie crust everywhere!" They both roared with laughter. They laughed and as they went through some other pics, they laughed even more. It was special to have a good friend, a very good friend, a bestie. Even in elder-age, it was important, though many thought this girlfriend thing to be more a teen deal. No not really. Not even a millennial thing…no, older women (and guys too) need a friend. Someone with whom they can be themselves, someone they trust. Sometimes it might just be your blood sister, but more often than not, women have girlfriends. Maybe they're our real and better angels?

Melodious found her multi-colored wallet happily lying on the kitchen table (full of money) next to the jean-jacket she was *going* to wear but had changed her mind and chosen the fleece. She left the money for Whiplash, took her jacket and her humbled-self up to her bedroom, sat down in her rocker and tried to remember forgetting. I totally forgot, she murmured to herself, I just didn't remember! I need to get a ride over to Thee Café to get my car. Later, I'll go later. Instead she put on her headset set and got steeped in the Blues.

++

Astra was not going to be bested by disappointment or disarray with her friends. No, she was going to plan her Advent and Christmas even if by herself. It was always fun and prayerful, Advent, powerful readings from the Scriptures during her devotion time. Always a time to take extra care as the winter set in and accidents could happen, and many folks began feeling a bit blue. The virus had done so many horrid things to people all over the County, not to say anything about the world last year that folks were happy they could come out this year and meet together.

There was her Wednesday quilting group who would meet just to make Christmas ornaments this year and she decided to go. There she would create her best work ever. She had only been quilting for about four years and did not do it every day so she needed to brush up. This year it was angels she wanted to highlight throughout her Advent, awaiting the *Herald of Good News Angel*, who would bring the message of the Child to the Wise. Yes angels. Little ones, cute ones, strong ones and bold; quilted ones were only a part of her plan. She was going to make angels for her tree from cotton balls right out of the field, designer clothespins, cardboard, Styrofoam, ribbon, plaster-of-paris, wood, painted rocks, sticks and material. She even had some stained glass bits as well as cork and pinecones. This tree and all her decorations would begin with just one tiny angel and end with a big Angel on top of the tree, the *Herald of Good News*. (in future referred to simply as *Harold*). Harold would be quilted and strong and he would have a long scroll in his hands announcing some pretty important news. All the lesser angels would be in the sky, as it were, zooming around him, bobbing on wires cut just for their flying, and encouraging him to bring the Message. There would be stars everywhere as well. Harold was very important in the scheme of things. Astra was also very fond of her Guardian Angel, Belinda. More of her later.

++

Percy and Beatrice were playing with Nevaeh. She had learned a rather complicated math game at school and wanted help. Neither Percy nor Beatrice had math at the top of their list of successes so they phoned Astra to come over and help figure out the game. It was a great visit but in the end Nevaeh scratched her head, looked at these older women, laughed, and went to her room. No one figured it out. She'd wait until she went back to school.

++

Whiplash, Melodious and Sarahfinna were at Thee Café First Sunday of Advent all smiles. They had quickly made up from their recent spat and now just wanted to eat. Astra and Alcor were on their way. Everyone was into angels! What a Christmas this would be! Why the whole town would be filled with angels. There would be no angel contest, though the town loved contests. There would just be various shops in town who agreed to have a certain number of angels on display. Thee Café and SueSue wanted as many as Astra and friends could make or collect.

Thee Café was still looking so new after the make-over the previous spring and filling it with wonderful colorful angels would just do the seasonal trick. SueSue had a Christmas tree up in the corner, not yet decorated, as she was awaiting her grandkids to come from North Carolina. They were thirteen, sixteen, boy and girl, and loved their granSue, and she loved them. They were the adopted children of her daughter, a pediatrician in private practice. Dr. MarySue Brinkly (unmarried) found them literally on her office steps one night, crying and whimpering as loudly as they could. They were clearly not twins, the girl nearly three she figured, but the boy a newborn, wrapped very tightly in blankets so they could not get out of the box. Whoever left them there must have been sure someone would find them in time. Dr.

MarySue gathered them up, took them into her office, examined each, and found food. She prepared soft sweet places for sleep and rocked them gently in her rocker, hugging them tightly trying to communicate safety and love. What to do next? She phoned Officer Dan who came by and wrote up a report. To make a long story short…no one ever claimed them, and no one was ever found having delivered them there. Eventually Dr. Sue was able to adopt them and they became a forever family. SueSue was thrilled and could not wait until December 19 when they were to arrive just in time for the Christmas Lecture gathering on December 20.

++

Astra went to her little library of resource books and began reading. There were things about angels she hadn't ever remembered forgetting so she was glad that this part of her devotional reading time was filled with new knowledge and joy! She discovered a fellow named Romanos the Melodist who wrote this about the Christmas miracle:

> 'The virgin today brings into the world the Eternal
> And the earth offers a cave to the Inaccessible.
> The angels and shepherds praise Him
> And the magi advance with the Star,
> For You are born for us,
> Little Child, God eternal.'(Kontakion).

Angels are spiritual and non-corporeal (ie no body); that is the name of their <u>office</u>, not their nature. Essentially, they are servants and messengers of God. Scripture reminds us angels 'always behold the face of My Father who is in heaven…the mighty ones who do God's Word…' They are spiritual but have intelligence and will and they are personal, immortal, and they surpass us in perfection. Wow pondered Astra.

182

They have quite a big job. The splendor of their glory bears witness to God. Oh my. Astra knew she knew so little but wanted to be able to converse with some confidence on the subject, a great believer in sharing things and knowledge our Astra. This would be no different. She just wrote down what she researched and kept the notes in her quilting box.

They are *His* angels as Jesus, the Christ, the birthday we celebrate at Christmas, is the center of the 'angelic world'.

That seems so obvious Astra noted when she began her reading again the next day. Jesus made angels the messengers of His divine plan. Angels have been present since creation and continue working God's plan of salvation. Just look at how they closed the Garden of Eden; protected Lot; saved Hagar and her child; kept Abraham's knife away from his son; communicated the law by their ministry; led the People of God; announced births and callings; and assisted the prophets. Whadda list. Astra was writing as fast as she could think. Gabriel came on the scene to announce both the birth of John the Baptist and that of Jesus Himself. Let's see what else? Who is going to understand all this? Astra thought, her own brain fizzing a bit. Oh, the songs of praise all the angels rendered at the birth of Jesus: *GLORY TO GOD IN THE HIGHEST*! They are still singing that song! Because Jesus is at the center, they were on duty to protect Him when He was born. They even helped Him in the desert, and held Him during His agony in the garden. Angels will come with Him when He returns because they will be announcing it! They must be the horn- tooting angels or the 'hear ye, hear ye' announcing angels. I think if a whole flock (are they a flock or a ...?) swooped down over our town I would have an immediate cardiac arrest. Astra was a bit dramatic but incredulous as well. I mean how do people know all these things about angels anyway? The Bible does cite a few specific examples but the rest...? Oh, well. I'll keep at my study. Gosh, thought Astra, angels are just pretty much like everywhere and I know I have a guardian angel who takes good care of me! My guardian angel is 'Belinda'. Is that sacrilegious? she wondered. Anyway Belinda is always there protecting me. Why once I broke some ribs, very painful and I was complaining to Belinda as to why she hadn't protected me better. A day or two later she 'asked' me if <u>both</u> sides of my ribs were broken. I answered 'no' and she pointed out it was because her wing was lying across <u>that</u> side. Really? So every day I thank her and ask her to stay close since I'm such a fraidy-cat. But Harold, where is Harold in all this and what will I put on the scroll in his hand when I finish quilting him?

++

Astra began preparing for the Christmas lecture at '*the dogwood*'. This year it would be about the Star, her favorite topic. (Likely, after all this study, angels may appear in there somewhere.) You probably remember Lecture #9 the year of the find of the Mississippi Agate? No? well it's documented elsewhere in this book. This Lecture series was way down the road a few years from that lecture (the last one she'd given) and now they were just called the Christmas Lecture, or the Summer Lecture, or the Easter Lecture... She had not given the Christmas Lecture before and being a slightly retired astronomer, they asked her to tell them all about the Christmas Star, allegedly shining over the cave where Jesus was born, guiding the Wise people to Him. She agreed. Astra had her own feelings about this Star and she had a good friend, David, an astronomer, who would also give her lots of material to share on the night.

++

Nevaeh hadn't stopped growing and her move from tween to teen not unremarkable. She thought to hand make all her Christmas presents secretly in her room this year. At the moment she had no idea how many she actually needed because there were so many people she loved and wanted to gift. Her bed stood above the ground so it would be a perfect place to hide her work. Of course, Astra's dog, Dog, might come over and nose around or Rockwell's dog, Fax could tear things up. She would just have to keep her door closed. Alcor's fish, Ivory and Hiccup, and her little turtle Mizar would not create any difficulty. They would not be coming by. Nevaeh's closet was chock-a-block full of stuff. You know, clothes, toys, papers, old school work, a basketball, her marvelous marble collection, including one she made herself over in Tuscaloosa, (see *THE DOGWOOD MARBLE JUBILEE* story) and who knows what else. It seemed this stuff had been there all of her thirteen years. She also had a long plastic container on wheels that would slide nicely under her bed and could keep the prezzies hidden and secure. Nevaeh rolled it out and quickly shoved the closet door shut and pushed with her bottom so nothing would fall out. Otherwise, she might have to clean the closet!

++

You might remember ChaChalita, the Argentinian dancer, Roz who has false teeth that frequently fall out of place, Joyous in the purple electric wheelie and Angel with her pink powered hair and copper colored skin? No? Well they were all in the quilting class that became a club. Anyway they will tell the story of the 'Three Wise Ones' better (maybe?) than the original. Astra had worked out the sky maps of stars and their configurations for years. Whiplash confronted her with questions.

"Why are you so into this Star thing anyway?" she asked, going over Astra's designs and peering into all her rolled up charts.

"I'm giving the Christmas Lecture at '*the dogwood*' in a couple of short weeks," she reminded her, "and I have a lot to plot."

"What's to plot? There was either a Star or there wasn't. Right?"

"Well, I suppose so, but despite your skepticism I can tell you something about the winter sky that night, over those days, and perhaps enlighten you? (Get it...en *light* en...never mind!).

Whiplash looked at her as if she were barmy. Why do people get into these weird things? Why the only thing I am really interested in is my *MARVEL* comic collection. Right. That's surely not weird. You read that correctly. Yes, I'm an 'old' lady but I love my *MARVELS*. Those are real adventurers and the superhero/ines are, well, super. I've got them back to the 40's (some I bought when I began my genuine collection). Melodious and Sarahfina still think I am a bit extreme, but what do they do? Why Melodious sings flat with her odd music and Sarafina has no collection of anything except complaints about our collections! Whew.

"So are you coming to the Lecture?" Astra asked.

"Might. Gotta go now. Later gator." And off she went. Astra could only smile and be grateful for having such a variety of wonderful friends!

++

ChaChalita had lived in the USA for over thirty years. When she first arrived, she lived with an uncle (Tio) Lorenzo. He was the brother of her father who was a dance instructor in Buenos Aires. Well, that's what they said, but the story was he was really a spy and his family was always in danger. Who knew? ChaChalita had the opportunity to come the USA to a dance competition when she was around thirteen (and she won third place) and her Tio Lorenzo whisked her away to safety. She never returned to Argentina and she never heard from her father again. Maybe he was a spy? Who for? Why? Who knows? Anyway, Tio moved house (down to the Deep South) and that's how she got to our County. We might very quietly mention that her documentation is still a bit flimsy at best. ChaChalita and Astra became friends some years ago, before the quilt club, and Astra wanted her to help with the set-up for the Lecture.

They met at Thee Café for the *red-white-and-blue plate* to discuss the project. While they were there in came Roz and Angel looking for a lunch beyond all lunches. Thee Café was just the (only) place. Having been made-over in the Spring (see *THEE CAFÉ MAKEOVER*) Roz said she lost her teeth less frequently, or was it more frequently, anyway because of the sheer beauty of the place? Angel had recently had her pink-powered hair dusted and she was feelin' fine, oh yes, very fine. Why, she was the very 'subject' of the day, bein' an *Angel* and all. She had a bit of that Dolly Parton look but with beautiful copper skin. How she got it to pile up that high was a mystery to most but she had her hairdresser's secrets tucked under her sloping bright gray hat (with red sequined hatband). The three of them could get up to some very interesting things. Astra knew that they could quilt beautifully and though she enjoyed it, she was not as professional. They were the ones to make her artistic ideas come to fruition. Astra was always happy to see them and gave a big 'hey' wave as they passed by on their way to the back to order from Jose and Kisha. Neither wanted the *red-white-and-blue plate* (that day it was mac 'n cheese, butter beans, and baked chicken, with peach cobbler). No. Roz wanted mashed potatoes, squash, and a little piece of grilled fish. All soft and her teeth tended to stay in place. Angel ordered a taco salad with all the perks and an order of fries, no salt. Whadda hoot. They found a booth near to ChaChalita and Astra and parked.

++

Nevaeh had been to the library and checked out the resources she needed for a report in her World History class. Of course, she could *google* it all on her tablet but she liked the feel of books. She had been assigned Israel and looked forward to learning something she didn't know much about. Every day the newspapers and social media were full of something about some country, usually at war. Israel had become its own country in 1947, the boundary lines drawn by the UN. The Palestinians did not have their own country yet. She thought that was unfair in the extreme. Could she find out WHY? Maybe that is a good place to start for a report. Work underway.

++

It was less than two weeks until the Lecture and Astra had gotten behind in her research. Yes, she'd done these sorts of talks before but this time she wanted to present something a bit new, if she could find it. She had agreed to meet Roz, Angel, ChaChalita, and Joyous, yes, at Thee Café for lunch. Each of them had agreed to make something about stars or angels to use as a part of the décor for 'the dogwood'. Astra had given them some ideas but what they created was far and away above expectations. Astra was over the moon! (well…).

The *red-white-and-blue plate* had a new twist. Jose had been experimenting with various Mexican dishes (kinda one at a time) over the past few months and besides a favorite of taco salad he had one day a week (Thursdays) he called the rest Hispanic Panic (and it became the *red-yellow-and green plate*) . The panic part was because as soon as he put any of it on the serving line, it was gone, gobbled up! The people in the long line loved his food and had a panic because …gosh, well, you get it. (They got nothing). Anyway, today was Hispanic Panic and Astra wanted a plate. She was fortunate to arrive in time and the plate had two soft tacos/beef or chicken, rice or beans, pico de gallo, a scoop of guacamole, and a lovely slice of flan. ($5 for seniors just like the *red-white-and-blue plate*). Each week was slightly different. Astra, Joyous, and ChaChalita each ordered one. Roz and Angel got something else. When Thee Café was made-over, they left one section of the biggest room with the longer tables so people could have meetings. Astra and friends brought their food there and began.

"Now I'd love to see what y'all have created," she began. Folks looked around at each other not being sure who should go first, and who might be embarrassed and the like. "Ah, come on now, y'all are great artists, that's why I asked y'all to *hep* me!" Astra beamed as they fumbled with their bags and boxes and soon one by one began to share their work.

Joyous rolled over to Astra's chair (designed in deep purples and white blocks by David Morris who ran the auto shop in town) and held up a mobile of splendid stars. It must have been over three feet long and besides the breathtaking stars that dangled below on various sorts of lines there were tiny lights and wee little bells that tingled in the air wafted by the stars movements. Everyone clapped. It was awesome. Astra could see that hanging from the ceiling.

ChaChalita's was a very large and beautifully quilted angel. The angel had hair with a flowing bright blue and silver scarf that moved with the energy of a dance. Roxie, the angel, had a long pale violet dress full of sparkles and marvelous soft-feathered wings. The quilt was 3D and ChaChalita had packed the high- heeled spiked silver shoes with extra wadding so they stuck out. Brilliant! Folks took a deep breath, oooed and aahhhed...

Roz had been quite a seamstress when young and wasn't back to it until she joined the quilt club several years ago. What she had discovered wasn't so much the sewing part but the 'I <u>like</u> sewing' part came back. Roz had made a long runner for the table featuring the Star and three Wise Ones as she called them. There were angels soaring around the Star and there were camels as seen from the back as if they were moving towards their destination. The room and table would be greatly embellished where food would appear in abundance.

Finally, Angel took her time getting her work out of a bag. She seemed as if she did not want to show it as it was rather big, rolled up, and folks couldn't quite see what it might be. Angel asked Whiplash, who had just walked in, to hold one end of it and they unrolled a painting of the town. It was amazing. All the businesses of the town were there in a modern abstract sorta way...not just primary-school painting, store after store. There were even some Churches, the hospital and the new addition to the High School. It was about 5' x 8' and would fit the wall space exactly behind the speaker's podium. Astra was stunned. It was really simple, colorful, crisp and very outside the box for Angel. She had clearly tried something new and became more receptive of adulation as the moments passed. The décor for the Lecture was going to *wow* those who came. Angel decided she might even paint another picture one day.

There was only one week left (the Lecture was scheduled for the end of the third week of Advent, December 20, a Saturday) and so Astra was completing her notes and being sure that those who wanted to come could get tickets. They were only $5 but that went into *THE DOGWOOD STARS SCIENCE CENTER FUND* (you see why they just call it '*the dogwood*'?) supporting the students with supplies, trips and the like for that semester. She was also very interested in reading Nevaeh's report on Israel.

++

Nevaeh had begun her report on Israel and the Palestinians showing how unfair she thought the whole question of territory was. One thing she mentioned, she had not known, was that Jesus was a Palestinian Jew. Bethlehem was in the Palestinian area. The many sights of the Holy Land interested her but the wars and bombs scared her. She showed a couple of pictures of the children afraid and starving. Then Nevaeh reported this: "*Where is the Child who has been born King of the Jews? We observed His Star at its rising and have come to pay Him homage.*"(Mt2:2) This was the question of the Wise Ones for Herod. Herod did not know and sent them on a mission to find Him. They went. They never went back to that 'horrid Herod' as she called him. Nevaeh hadn't gotten further than that and was glad the report was not due until after the Christmas break. She was, however, very happy to have seen the conjunction of Jupiter and Saturn, amazed at what she could view with the naked eye. Of course, she also saw it with Astra Fisic's telescope out in her backyard. Wonder if that was how the Christmas Star appeared?

++

Dr. Hanna Edana, Director of 'the 'dogwood' rolled over to the podium, parked her bright orange electric-wheelie and asked the audience for their attention. She welcomed folks and talked a bit about the work of the Center over the past few months, well, since the Easter Lecture, last April. Then Dr. Hanna thanked Roz, ChaChalita, Angel and Joyous for their amazing artistic decorations for the special night. Folks clapped and the quartet was chuffed. None of them had really been out front before and Astra was happy to do it. Hanna introduced Astra who came over to the podium. Hanna rolled over to her spot.

Sarafina read from Luke's Gospel to begin the session before Astra began her talk:

"For while gentle silence enveloped all things and night in its swift course was now half gone, Your all-powerful Word leaped from heaven, from Your royal throne." (Lk2:51) Except for the tiny reading light on the podium, the hall went dark and Astra's power point filled the ceiling with the winter night sky. Pop. Pop. Pop. Folks who had a home Church were more likely familiar with that Scripture than others but they all listened attentively anyway. There was a focused silence in the room and folks settled in to hear what Astra had discovered.

"Venus is first to appear in the evening and last to disappear in the morning (she showed them where it was)…was it a replacement Star westward-leading that brought the Magi to Jerusalem with a question for Herod?" Astra began unrolling her maps and charts and pointed to this and that in the night winter sky. Folks strained their necks trying to see. The power point projections were easier to take in. After she had shown pictures of star constellations and the like she added, "I don't think there was a constellation, or conjunction of planets. Here's why: the Star moved and the Star was not about an astronomical thing but about Jesus, the Messiah, the long-awaited, the coming of the Light, drawing even the Gentile world to Him. Its radiance perhaps showed that Jesus would come for everyone...not just the Jews....Let's look at a little bit of Isaiah." Dr. MarySue's son, Devin, arose, came to the podium and read beautifully.

> *"Rise up in splendor! Your light has come, the glory of the Lord shines upon you. See, darkness covers the earth... but on you the Lord shines, and over you appears His glory. Nations shall walk by your light, and royalty by your shining radiance...you shall be radiant at what you see, your heart shall throb and overflow...caravans of camels shall fill you. Dromedaries from Midian and Ephah; all from Sheba shall come bearing gold and frankincense, and proclaiming the praises of the Lord...You shall know that I am your Savior, your Redeemer; I will appoint peace your governor and justice your ruler. No longer will violence be heard of in your land...the Lord shall be your Light forever, your God shall be your glory...the days of mourning shall be at an end...I the Lord will accomplish these things when their time comes. (Is 60:1-3)*

Devin stood quietly for a moment and then went back to his seat. Astra continued.

"Before I tell y'all *my* theory of the Star I want you to hear the report my very good friend, David, the astronomer, sent me. His research and professional opinion point to this:

"The main problem of figuring out the Star mentioned in Matthew's Gospel is first determining when Christ was <u>actually</u> born. There are a few clues here. Christ was born in the time of Herod. Herod died near the time of a lunar eclipse. There was a lunar eclipse visible in the Middle East in 4 BC. That would place the birth of Christ a few years *before* Christ. Also, Joseph and Mary were traveling while pregnant to pay a census tax. There was a census tax needed by Caesar again giving clues that Christ must have been born a few years BC.

Another question is who were the Wise Men? They were from the east, Persia perhaps. They were therefore Gentiles and likely astrologers who were looking for clues in the sky of the coming of a Jewish Messiah. So what would they look for?

Possibilities:

1. Some sort of *miracle*. If that, no explanation could scientifically be made.

2. *Supernova*, a bright, exploding star. That initially sounds great, BUT, there are no records of such in the sky around this time. The Chinese astrologers watched the sky carefully for signs regarding their rulers. Plus everybody would have seen this. Apparently, only the Wise Men saw this Star, so it was likely not a supernova.

3. *Comet*. Likely not, as comets were seen historically as bad omens, foretelling the fall of kings and dynasties, not the births of them.

4. *Meteor*. Nope, happens too fast to lead anyone anywhere!

5. *Planets*. Best bet. In 4, 3, and 2 BC there was a triple conjunction of Venus and Jupiter. This means that they lined up three different times. From an astrologer's point of view, this would be very significant. Jupiter is named after the 'King of the Gods', Venus is the 'Goddess of love, beauty, and fertility', and the conjunction happened near the star Regulus in Leo the Lion.

The lion is the 'King of the beasts' and Regulus is named the 'King Star'. This conjunction would have been visible to all, but to the Wise Men, who were looking for a <u>sign in</u> the sky, this could have been the sign to travel towards finding this Messiah. It would have taken these Wise Men months to make this journey from Persia to Judea. So for these reasons, an alignment of Jupiter and Venus, along with the Star Regulus *may* have been the Star that guided the Magi. Visible to all, but only significant if one was *looking* for a sign. Planetary groupings were likely the cause of this Star..."

Astra stood in silence. The very interested folks who had gathered were also stilled. "Isn't David a smart fellow? I am so grateful for his hard work. He was not able to join us tonight as he is over in Virginia. Early in Advent, I discovered a reading I had totally forgotten. Way back in Numbers 24:17ff...we find:

"I see him, though not now; I behold him, though not near: a star shall advance from Jacob and a staff shall rise from Israel..." Maybe, as the Fathers thought, it was not directly connected to the magi Star...but was it a messianic prophecy?"

"Now I will share with you my very own theory about that Star Light. Go back to the Isaiah reading...and remember what he said in more than one way:

"on you <u>the Lord shines</u>, and over you appears His glory... the <u>Lord shall be your Light</u> forever, your God shall be your glory... or consider the opening lines in St. John's Gospel: *"Whatever came to be in Him, found life, life for the Light of all. The Light shines in the darkness, a darkness that did not overcome it."* (Jn1: 4-5).*

I think that Star was a way for our sweet Lord to artistically express His presence so the Wise would not get lost in their seeking. May I suggest the Star was indeed the Lord God? The Light? That the Star was a manifestation of God? Emmanuel? God-with-Us? God continues to this day to fill our skies with amazing stars, the highway to heaven (in Japan), for example, that lines up once a year with the road, so that we can find our way (she showed them a power point of that amazing road)." Astra waited, she heard some ahas… "We also have to consider that since the Scriptures are not 'history' as such that the Wise ones may not have visited the Child until He was beyond two after they came back from Egypt where they had been refugees from Herod? You will have to make a decision yourself about what you think. I have given you David's best research, my own theory and now before we leave in peace be reminded of the other wonderful gift this Star brought to those who sought the Messiah and continue to do so: JOY!

"*There, ahead of them went the Star that they had seen at its rising, until it stopped over the place where the Child was. When they saw that the Star had stopped they were overwhelmed with JOY!*" (Mt2:9-10*)* "That is what I put on the scroll for Harold, the *Herald of Good News,* to be reading (and announcing) as he sits atop my tree." Astra smiled as folks clapped and scratched their heads, shrugging their shoulders and looking at one another. "Our very atoms come from those stars, so we are one with stardust! Remember God is Light and in God there is no darkness."

What to say now? Let's eat seemed appropriate. And they did.

THE END

CPSIA information can be obtained
at www.ICGtesting.com
Printed in the USA
JSHW052016010621
15423JS00001B/10